"I ASKE[...] [...] of your[...]

Emma glared at him. "What are you going to do if I don't?"

Brent shoved a hand through his hair, disheveling it. Emma was driving him crazy. In twenty-four hours he had ping-ponged back and forth between the longing to turn her over his knee and the desire to kiss away the memory of every four-letter word she knew. The threat of washing her mouth out with soap hadn't fazed her, so maybe it was time to change tactics. "The next four-letter word that comes out of your mouth, I'm going to kiss you until you've completely forgotten it."

The curse that slipped from Emma's mouth was purely accidental, or so she told herself.

Brent reached out and hauled her against his chest. "That does it," he said, and his mouth swooped down onto hers with deadly accuracy.

WHAT ARE *LOVESWEPT* ROMANCES?

They are stories of true romance and touching emotion. We believe those two very important ingredients are constants in our highly sensual and very believable stories in the LOVE-SWEPT line. Our goal is to give you, the reader, stories of consistently high quality that may sometimes make you laugh, sometimes make you cry, but are always fresh and creative and contain many delightful surprises within their pages.

Most romance fans read an enormous number of books. Those they truly love, they keep. Others may be traded with friends and soon forgotten. We hope that each LOVESWEPT romance will be a treasure—a "keeper." We will always try to publish

LOVE STORIES YOU'LL NEVER FORGET
BY AUTHORS YOU'LL ALWAYS REMEMBER

The Editors

EMMA AND THE HANDSOME DEVIL

MARCIA EVANICK

BANTAM BOOKS

NEW YORK · TORONTO · LONDON · SYDNEY · AUCKLAND

EMMA AND THE HANDSOME DEVIL
A Bantam Book / June 1995

If you would be interested in receiving protective vinyl covers for your Loveswept books, please write to this address for information:

Loveswept
Bantam Books
P.O. Box 985
Hicksville, NY 11802

ISBN 0-553-44467-0

Published simultaneously in the United States and Canada

Bantam Books are published by Bantam Books, a division of Bantam Doubleday Dell Publishing Group, Inc. Its trademark, consisting of the words "Bantam Books" and the portrayal of a rooster, is Registered in U.S. Patent and Trademark Office and in other countries. Marca Registrada. Bantam Books, 1540 Broadway, New York, New York 10036.

PRINTED IN THE UNITED STATES OF AMERICA
OPM   0 9 8 7 6 5 4 3 2 1

To my niece, Jessica,
Cherish these moments and
spread your wings.

ONE

Emma Carson gently nudged another chicken out of her way as she grappled with the fifty-pound bag of feed hoisted on her shoulder. A curse that would have made her older brothers proud tumbled from her lips as another chicken went squawking between her feet, causing her to stagger the remaining steps to the feed bins. In her opinion chickens were the stupidest animals God had ever seen fit to put on this earth. They even lacked the intelligence to get out of her way when she was trying to feed them. She carefully set the bag down, making sure none of the witless creatures were under it, and slashed the coarse burlap with the lethal looking knife she always carried in her back pocket. She automatically measured the feed into the bins, ignoring the clucking and strutting of the hundred or so chickens that surrounded her.

The unusual heat spell sweeping through Arkansas had sent the temperature soaring into the high nineties all week. Emma couldn't remember a hotter April in Strawberry Ridge. It seemed as if the gates of hell had been flung open and the devil was on the prowl. Emma chuckled for the first time in weeks. How appropriate that the heat had scorched the land in preparation for the devil's arrival. The devil was scheduled to show up any day now, or so his telegram had announced. Emma had been shocked by the telegram the previous week. She had never received a telegram in her life, but she instinctively knew they bore bad news. Hers hadn't been an exception. The devil was on his way, and his name was Brent Haywood. He was also half owner of the Amazing Grace Farm. She was the other half—the half that had been doing all the work.

Emma slowly made her way out of the chicken run and back to the battered pickup truck. She filled two buckets from the tank full of water sitting in the truck's bed. Her shoulders ached, her back was sore, and the muscles in her arms protested as she hoisted the two buckets and made her way over to the water troughs. For months she had been running the farm on her own, working eighteen-hour days. Still, every morning when she hauled herself out of bed before dawn, the list of chores had grown longer.

When she had graduated from high school seven years earlier, the only job she'd been able to find was the one no one else wanted, working for

Levi James. Old Levi had a reputation for being tough as horseshoes, more disagreeable than a porcupine, and impossible to work for. Over the years, Emma had found all of that true and a lot more, but she'd also discovered something else. Levi had a heart of gold. Of course, she had never told him that for fear of losing her job, but she had shown old Levi how much he had meant to her during the last two months of his life. During those months she had nursed him at home when he refused to go to the hospital, and she had run the farm. Levi must have returned some of those feelings, because when he had made his will two years before he even took ill, he had left her half the farm. Emma had been shocked when the lawyer had driven all the way out from town to the farm the day after Levi died to give her the news. She had expected to be looking for another job and would have bet the price of a new pair of boots that Levi's only daughter, Julie, would inherit the seventy-two-acre farm. Of course, Julie had hated the farm so much, she had taken off the day she graduated from high school and had only been back once in the more than thirty years since then. Emma, though, had inherited half the farm; Levi's grandson, Brent Haywood, had inherited the other half. Levi's daughter had received only a small mention in the will. Something to the effect of "Julie, you wanted nothing to do with me or this farm all those years ago, so you shall have your wish and receive nothing now." No one had ever claimed Levi was a forgiving man.

Emma finished filling the water troughs and ran an expert glance around the enclosed area. She studied the chickens and gauged them to have about another four weeks before she could ship them off to the meat packers. Raising free-range chickens was a lot more time-consuming than breeding conventional broilers. Broilers could be shipped off to packers when they were anywhere between seven and twelve weeks old. Free-range chickens, though, weren't injected with hormones to speed up growth, or bombarded with a multitude of antibiotics to ward off diseases. People were finally realizing what all those chemicals were doing to their food, and were willing to pay extra for healthy, drug-free, natural chickens. Levi had scoffed at her idea of raising free-range chickens at first, but he had come around about a year earlier. He had even gone as far as to nickname the Barred Plymouth Rock hens "Prima Donnas."

Emma swiped the back of her hand over her eyes and removed any traces of moisture. She wouldn't cry now for Levi. She hadn't cried when the doctors had given him only months to live, and she hadn't cried as she'd watched him suffering day after day. She hadn't cried at the grave a few hundred yards from the house when they'd lowered him into the ground to lie in peace beside his wife, whom he'd lost over forty years ago. Tears had blurred her vision for a few moments when she'd glanced around at the mourners. Besides the minister and herself, there were two neighbors who had come out of curiosity, not respect. They were scoping out the land, Emma had guessed, deciding if it would make a nice addition to their own farm. She had suppressed a smile as they'd gallantly lowered the casket and started to shovel in the dirt. Levi had probably been laughing in heaven at their act of courtesy. He had known when he made out his will that Emma would never sell her half of the farm. His grandson was another matter. Emma had no idea what Brent Haywood would do with his half.

She wearily climbed back into the cab of the truck and slowly drove over ruts and ditches to the next enclosure of chickens. It was barely noon and she had been up and working for eight hours. Her old T-shirt, with the emblem of the local feed mill printed across the chest, was sticking to her back, and she had ripped another hole in her jeans while fixing the stuck carburetor on the truck. Her jeans had so many holes in them now, if she ripped another one or two she might as well feed the chickens in her undies. All her decent jeans were piled on the floor by the washer, along with just about everything else she owned. Tonight, after she plowed the ten-acre hay field, she just might get the chance to wash a load or two. That was, if she didn't fall asleep first. Laundry wasn't high on her list of priorities. Keeping the farm was.

Brent Haywood slowed the rental car as he passed through Strawberry Ridge. The quiet, small town, with its tree-lined streets and handful of stores, didn't stir any memories. Since he had only passed through Strawberry Ridge twice in his life— once on the way to his grandfather's farm and once when he left the farm—he hadn't expected it to. Sixteen years was a long time to remember a town he had only driven through.

Sixteen years was also a long time to remember a grandfather he had spent ten days with when he was twelve years old. His mother and husband number three had dropped him off on their way to Paris and their honeymoon. The housekeeper, Mrs. Butterfield, usually took care of him when his mother jetted from one continent to another. The day of his mother's wedding, though, Mrs. Butterfield had landed in the hospital with pneumonia, and Julie Haywood Montgomery Smyth had had no other recourse than to deposit her son on her father's doorstep unannounced. Brent could still remember the look on his grandfather's face when he had opened the door—anger, disappointment, and a yearning so deep that at first Brent had thought he had imagined it. Over the next ten days, though, he had seen how lonely his grandfather was. During the next couple of years Brent had sent his grandfather a few letters and cards, but never once received a reply. By the time he was sixteen and had discovered cars and girls, his grandfather was a distant memory. Only now, after his death, did Brent realize he should have tried harder, maybe even visited his grandfather once in a while, but life had a way of interfering.

The town of Strawberry Ridge faded in the rearview mirror, and Brent picked up the hand-drawn map his grandfather's lawyer had faxed him the week before with the directions to the Amazing Grace Farm. Brent still hadn't gotten over the shock of learning his grandfather had left him half the farm. The copy of the will he had received stated, "To my only grandchild, Brent, since half the blood running through your body is James blood, I leave you half the farm, half the assets, half the debts. Now let's see if you can do half the work." No fond memories, no words of love, just a challenge. A challenge he was going to accept.

Rolling wheat fields, towering silos, enormous barns, and rugged hills off in the distance greeted him for mile after mile. The farm was seven miles out of town along a highway that paralleled the Strawberry River. Every once in a while he could catch a glimpse of water sparkling in the late afternoon sunlight. If only it weren't so hot. He automatically reached for the air-conditioning lever and moved it into the deeper blue zone as the radio announcer proclaimed it was ninety-five degrees in the shade. Brent had nearly choked on the heat when he'd stepped out of the airport terminal in Little Rock. When he'd left New York that morning, it had been a refreshing fifty-six degrees, the leaves and grass in Central Park had been a brilliant green, and the dogwoods had been in bloom. Strawberry Ridge looked as though it had been baking in the blistering sun for at least six decades.

The sight of a battered mailbox leaning precariously to the left caught his attention. He stepped on the brakes when he saw the words *Amazing Grace Farm* painted on the box in faded red. The dirt lane that intersected the highway looked about as inviting as a blockade. He carefully maneuvered the car over the ruts to the crest of a hill. Below him, spread out like a quilt made by God, was the farm. The house, barn, and a couple of newer buildings sat at the end of the dirt road. Fields of hay were in various stages of growth, and in between the fields were enclosed areas with chicken coops and dozens of chickens running around. Sixteen years ago his grandfather had owned only about six chickens for fresh eggs, a cow for milk, and a couple of hogs for meat. It appeared his grandfather had made advances, at least in the working end of the farm, over the years.

Brent stepped out of the car and surveyed the farm. It looked worn and run-down. The small patch of lawn surrounding the house needed mowing, and the nearest things to flowers were the blooming weeds dotting the grass. The barn was the color of maroon mud, and the house hadn't been painted in this decade. It looked exactly as it had when he was twelve, only a little more beaten up from the years. He had hoped, after learning his grandfather had employed a hired hand seven years earlier, that some improvements had been made to the house. His hopes were dashed with one look.

Brent squinted against the lowering sun and spotted a rusty old tractor stirring up dust and dirt in a field far off to the right, near a ridge. Chickens pecked and scratched at the newly turned soil. If his memory served him right, the farm ran to the top of the ridge where a line of oak trees stood. His mysterious partner in the farm appeared to be busy. When he'd questioned the lawyer about who had inherited the other half of the farm, the response had been vague, something about the person who had been working for his grandfather. The lawyer never said how old the man was, if he had a family, or even his name.

Brent slowly climbed back into the cool car and rubbed the back of his neck, where tension was building. It looked as though the Amazing Grace Farm was going to take a lot of hard work and cash to turn it into the quiet retreat he so desperately needed. At twenty-eight he found himself at a crossroads in life, and he hadn't a clue as to which way to go. He'd always known his career as a model would be short-lived, and he had been saving for the end since the beginning. Inheriting half the farm had prompted him to give up the hectic schedule and the empty shell that had become his life.

When he was twenty-two and fresh out of college, he had been thrilled by the money, the big-shot advertising agencies fighting over him, and the hordes of women who literally threw themselves at him. Within months, though, the thrill had worn off and his modeling had turned from an adventure into a job. Over the years, the job had become a nightmare. Half the time he didn't know what city he was in, he saw less and less of his own apartment, he couldn't smile unless there was a camera pointed at him, and he was sick to death of total strangers combing his hair, straightening his clothes, and watching him change.

The women were the worst. Twice he had started into a serious relationship only to discover the woman of his dreams was using him to further her own career, or simply as an attractive escort to impress her friends. No one wanted to know who the real Brent Haywood was, and he was tired of shocking people when he opened his mouth and intelligent sentences came pouring out. Just because God had given him a handsome face and a nice body didn't mean that the Big Guy had short-changed him in the brain department.

Brent slowly drove to the house and parked the car. He stared at the crooked porch for a minute before realizing it wasn't an optical illusion. The porch had sunk to the right by a good eight inches. The closer he looked, the more it appeared his hopes of peace and tranquility were sinking faster than the porch. How was he ever supposed to figure out which direction to take in life when his new home was falling down on top of him? What in the hell kind of hired hand had his grandfather employed?

He cautiously stepped onto the porch and breathed a sigh of relief when the boards held. The screen door had a long rip in it, and half the flies in Arkansas were using it for a passageway into the house. He gave a loud knock and called, "Hello, anybody home?" before shooing away the flies and opening the door. His mouth fell open as he walked into the living room. If he hadn't known better, he would have sworn he had stepped into a time warp and been transported back sixteen years. Not one piece of furniture in the room had changed, not even the curtains.

Emma carefully drove the tractor into the middle of the barn and gently turned off the ignition. The old John Deere had seen better days, and between Levi and herself they had been nursing it along for the past ten years. By her calculations the Amazing Grace Farm would be able to afford a new tractor by the time Halley's comet passed by the earth again.

She climbed down out of the seat, and as she stretched her hands over her head to get the kinks out of her back, she considered the strange car parked in front of the house. It had caught her by surprise when she'd first seen it, until she'd realized it must belong to the grandson, Brent. She had expected the devil to arrive driving some hot, sexy red sports car, maybe a Firebird or something. Not the plain blue mid-size Chevy sitting out front. But then again, what did she know about the devil? In her mind she had labeled Brent a heartless devil for what he and his mother had done to Levi over the years. Levi hadn't deserved to die alone, without any member of his family around to comfort him during his last hours. But that was what had happened. Twice Emma had secretly called the only phone number Levi had for his daughter, and twice she had left messages on an answering machine. The first message was a plea for Julie to return her call, that there was a family emergency. The second message was blunt, to the point, and bordered on the threatening side. Julie had never returned either message.

Emma could feel the tension building in her shoulders and willed her muscles to relax. She reached her left hand way up in the air and bent her body toward the right, stretching the sore muscles from her arm down past her hips. Sitting on a bouncy tractor for the past four hours had jostled every bone in her body, never mind her teeth. She stretched her right hand up and proceeded to stretch out the other side of her aching body. In a minute she would have to introduce herself to the devil, and she preferred to do it not looking like the Hunchback of Notre Dame.

She interlaced her fingers, extended both hands over her head, and then swept them to the ground while bending at the waist. Her spine screamed half in agony, half in pleasure as she pressed her palms to the ground. Between her slightly parted legs, she could see the opened doorway she had just driven through. Early evening sunlight filled it, and she had to squint against the light. When the shadow of a man stepped into the doorway, she started and nearly lost her balance. So much blood had rushed to her head that when she jerked upward, everything went black for a second and she staggered.

The man rushed forward with an arm extended, ready to steady her. "Easy," he said.

Emma glanced at his hand as if it were a copperhead snake. The dirty wheel of the tractor bit into her back, and she automatically straightened the red baseball cap she was wearing. His golden tanned hand, with its neatly manicured fingernails, slowly lowered. She followed that movement with her gaze and studied the man before her. Soft leather shoes were lightly coated with dust from the barn floor. His khaki pants weren't skintight, but she was left without a doubt as to the size and shape of his legs. An expensive leather belt emphasized his narrow waist and the tightness of his stomach muscles. His short-sleeved white cotton shirt stretched across his chest and shoulders. Her glance shot upward to his face. A strong chiseled jaw with just a hint of a shadow was the perfect platform for his seductive mouth. His nose was flawless and his eyes appeared to be silver. He was the most gorgeous man she had ever seen.

A grimace pulled at her mouth, and she

straightened as her right hand casually slipped into the rear pocket of her jeans where she kept her knife. The man standing before her looked nothing like the photograph of the skinny, bucktoothed boy Levi had kept on his dresser. The only points of similarity were the brown hair and gray eyes.

"Who in the hell are you?" she asked.

He frowned and slowly raised his gaze from the front of her shirt to her face. "Shouldn't I be the one asking that?"

The weight of the knife felt comforting in the palm of her hand. She had noticed the way he stared at her unconfined breasts. It wasn't her fault every bra she owned was dirty, or that it had to be at least a hundred degrees out there and her T-shirt was clinging to her moist body like a second skin. The field had had to be turned so that it was ready for planting tomorrow, and nature really didn't care if she did it dressed like a nun or stark naked. Rain was coming in the next couple of days, and the seeds had to get in.

"Mister, you've got to the count of three to spill your name." She kept the knife behind her back as the blade sprang from its ivory handle. Levi's words came rushing back: *Never let your opponent see your weapon until it's too late.*

The gorgeous man glanced around the barn in amusement. "The name's Brent Haywood and I'm Levi's grandson and half owner of the Amazing Grace Farm." He offered a friendly smile. "Didn't you get my telegram?"

Emma slowly brought her hand out from behind her back. She watched as Haywood's eyes widened in shock at the sight of the knife. Expertly she flicked the blade back into its handle. Her smile held a lot of satisfaction. "You got your teeth fixed."

He frowned again as the knife disappeared into her back pocket. "Where did you get that thing?"

"Levi bought it for me for Christmas about five years ago." Pretty Boy seemed to have turned a mite green around the edges, she saw. "He figured as long as I was out shooting squirrels and possums for dinner, I might as well skin them too." She had never shot a squirrel or possum in her life, but Pretty Boy didn't know that. Now, an occasional fox was another matter. Chicken farmers had been plagued by foxes raiding coops about as long as there'd been chickens on earth. Levi had given her the knife and taught her how to use it for only one purpose, self-defense.

"You're pulling my leg, right?"

"Ain't touching your leg, Haywood." She gave him her best rendition of a country-bumpkin grin, regretting that she didn't have a wad of chewing tobacco that she could spit on the ground.

"The name's Brent, and you still haven't introduced yourself."

She normally would have yanked off her hat and been polite, but something about Haywood rubbed her the wrong way. Or maybe it was the fact that he was rubbing her the right way that caused her back to bristle. Any man who looked like he did belonged either on the covers of magazines or on the silver screen, not standing in her barn. "Name's Emma Jane Carson, half owner of the Amazing Grace Farm. You can call me Carson." She held out her hand without wiping off the dirt.

Brent gazed at the hand for a moment, then smiled. He reached out and gave her a hearty handshake. "Glad to make your acquaintance, Emma."

She grinned knowingly and released his hand. His grip had been firm, but there hadn't been one callus or blister on his palm. He had the hands of a rich man. "I'm not selling my half of the farm, so knock off the charm, city boy."

"I don't remember asking you to."

"It's coming."

"No, it's not." He glanced around the cluttered barn before looking back at her. "I was going to ask if it's all right that I put my bags in my grandfather's old bedroom."

"You might be more comfortable in town. There're two real nice bed-and-breakfasts back there." She hadn't given too much thought to sharing the house with Levi's grandson. His picture, taken when he was twelve, screamed one word, *Geek!* Emma had figured, once a geek, always a geek. Her gaze slid up his fabulous body and roamed his handsome face. Just goes to prove that sometimes even she was wrong. Brent Haywood didn't look like any geek she knew. In fact, the man looked like a movie star. Just what she didn't need.

A fancy peacock strutting his stuff around the house and spending his day in front of the bathroom mirror.

"Is there a problem with me staying in the house?" he asked.

"No, it's just that I don't have time for cleaning and cooking and such. This is a working farm." She let the last sentence hang in the air.

"And you've been doing all the work, haven't you?"

"Don't see no one else here, do you?"

"How long have you been doing all the work?"

"Honestly?"

"Partners should always be honest with each other."

Partners! She'd never thought of herself as someone's partner before. She had been a daughter, a sister, and a hired hand, but never a partner. Emma stared at the man standing before her and realized they were equals when it came to the farm. He had her beat hands-down in a beauty contest, and probably could outsmart her when it came to books, but where the farm was concerned, she was his equal. Lord, she had a peacock for a partner! "About a year ago Levi started to slow down, so I picked up the slack. He was bedridden for over two months at the end."

"I guess with the medical bills and help, there wasn't any money to hire on another hand."

Emma laughed and sadly shook her head.

Damn city boy didn't know squat about farming, especially a measly seventy-two acres. "Levi refused to go into the hospital, said if he was going to die, he was doing it on his own land. The doctor usually stopped by every other day or so."

"Who took care of him?"

"Doesn't take a rocket scientist to change a bedpan or dish out pills."

"Why didn't you hire a nurse?"

"Look around you, city boy." She glanced down at her own attire and grimaced. "Does it look like I can afford to hire a nurse?"

"What about his insurance? Surely it covered home care."

Emma chuckled. "Insurance? What planet have you been living on? Haven't you heard there's a health care crisis in this country?"

"Do you mean to tell me my grandfather didn't have health insurance?"

"Levi would have had to remortgage the farm to afford the premiums. That was something he would never do. This farm meant more to him than any piece of paper guaranteeing him health care. Health care, I might add, that wouldn't have saved his life anyway. It might have prolonged it by a couple of weeks if he was hooked up to machines and tubes." She couldn't prevent the small shivers that shook her body. "If you had taken the time to know your grandfather, you would have known he didn't want to die that way."

Brent's gaze was riveted to her face. "How did he die?"

Emma's chin rose a notch and she had to force her voice not to break. "Cancer." Over the years, she had grown to love Levi like a grandfather. She'd never known any of her own grandparents, and Lord knows her father didn't stir any emotions in her besides disgust. She had come to think of Levi not only as her employer but as a friend and family.

"The lawyer told me he had cancer," Brent said. "I want to know how he died."

"It was a Friday morning," Emma began, hoping she could get through this without crying, "and he was cursing the pain and cursing his inability to help me plow the twenty acres to the west. I tried to feed him breakfast and he refused. His appetite was gone, but his mind was semiclear, if the curses he was stringing together were any indication." She swiped at the tears clinging to her lashes. "I left him sitting up in the hospital bed that I had borrowed and placed in front of his bedroom window, so he could watch me plow that damn field." Tears were now rolling freely down her cheeks, and she gave up trying to hide them. "When I returned around lunchtime, he was clutching a framed picture of his wife taken the day they got married. He died peacefully and alone, just as he wanted."

Brent roughly cleared his throat and took a step closer. "Emma?"

She turned away and headed for the open doorway. "Now, if you will excuse me, *partner*, I haven't eaten since five this morning."

Brent stood in the shadows of the barn and watched as she walked out into what was left of the sunlight.

TWO

Brent shuddered as Emma opened a can of spaghetti and sauce and plopped the entire mass into a saucepan. "Is that your dinner?"

She took a fork and broke the lump apart. "Yeah, it's the maid's day off and I have to fend for myself." She speared a long noodle, wrapped it around the fork, and popped it into her mouth. "Life can be a bitch sometimes."

A dark flush of anger swept up his cheeks. How could one small package of a woman wreak so much havoc with his emotions? Not ten minutes ago, in the barn, he'd wanted to pull her into his arms and comfort her. Now he felt like throttling her for being such a smart-mouth. His gut was telling him that Emma was enjoying playing the country hayseed. He had given her a couple of minutes to compose herself before following her back to the house. He had found her in the kitchen, and her act of composure seemed to have been throwing water on her face and washing her hands.

Under the harsh glare of the kitchen light he got his first good look at her. He couldn't label her a classic beauty because her nose was a trifle wide and her mouth was too generous. But her cheekbones were high, and she had the clearest blue eyes he had ever seen. Emma had a natural beauty that was more potent because she hadn't done anything to enhance it. She had left her dusty baseball cap along with her dirty boots in the mudroom at the back of the house. Underneath the cap had been a thick braid of golden hair. The end, held together by a rubber band, swung halfway down her back as she moved around the kitchen, teasing his senses. He had an incredible urge to undo the braid and sink his fingers into the silky mass.

Furious with himself for thinking about Emma as a woman instead of a partner, he rummaged through the cabinets, looking for something decent to eat. He had been amazed when he had stepped into the barn to introduce himself to his new partner, only to discover a pert denim-covered bottom bouncing in the air, with Emma's face peering at him upside down from between her knees. His partner was a woman, a very attractive woman. He hadn't counted on that.

He grabbed a can of chili. Considering there were only six cans in the entire cabinet, he didn't have a whole lot to choose from. "Can I borrow some food?"

"Sure. I paid for it out of the profits."

He saw her glance at the clean bowls sitting in the dish drainer before she picked up the bubbling pan of spaghetti and a fork. She sat down on one of the stools and started to eat directly from the pan.

Brent shook his head and turned his back so she wouldn't see his smile. He had noticed her longing glance at the dishes. Emma ate out of pans about as often as he did. For some reason she was insisting on the hayseed routine. He reached into the ancient refrigerator and pulled out two cans of soda. He handed one to her. "Maybe one of us should do some shopping tomorrow."

"It will have to be you. I have to plant ten acres of hay tomorrow." She finished off the spaghetti, downed half of the soda, and headed for the washer out in the mudroom.

Brent watched in amazement as she jammed in nearly a dozen pairs of jeans, poured out a capful of detergent, and slammed the lid shut. "If you leave me a list of what you would like," he said, "I guess I could do the shopping while you do the planting." The role reversal wasn't lost on him, but he wasn't foolish enough to suggest he do the planting. First, he had never driven a tractor, and second, and more important, he had never planted so much as a petunia in his life. He had grocery shopped plenty of times, though, and for some reason he didn't want to screw up this first duty as a partner. He had a gut feeling Emma was going to test him, time and time again.

"There's not a whole lot of money, so there's not a whole lot you can pick up." She glared at the rattling washing machine, as if daring it to act up, before walking back through the kitchen and into the living room. After a few minutes of rummaging through a paper-strewn desk, she returned to the kitchen with a blue journal.

"Here's the records." She handed the journal to Brent. "Every penny received so far this year and every penny spent has been recorded. Levi believed this was the easiest way to keep records for the accountant for when he had to figure out the taxes."

Brent took the book and grimaced when he saw the first entry, dated January 1. *Cash on hand $231.56.* How in the hell do you start a whole year with a lousy two hundred and thirty-one dollars? "Did Levi have a savings account?"

"No. At the end of every month he paid me, and if there was any money left, he gave himself a few bucks for clothes, personal items, etcetera."

Brent skimmed the list of entries until he came to Emma's and his grandfather's names. The pitiful amount next to Emma's name shook him. "Is that all he paid you for a month's work?" he asked, stunned.

"That's all I needed. He provided a room and meals, plus the use of the truck any time I needed it."

The amount next to his grandfather's name was smaller still. He flipped the pages until he came to the last entry, dated the previous Saturday. *Groceries*

$32.48. The final figure in the book was cash on hand. It was a little more than the beginning balance.

"He worked this farm his entire life, and this is what he had to show for it?" Brent wasn't disappointed by the amount; he hadn't been expecting any windfall. He was just shocked that a man could dedicate his life to something and have absolutely nothing to show for it at the end. In the world in which he had been raised, the only thing that counted was how much a person owned. Material possessions were everything. Money was nice and definitely came in handy, but through the years he had come to realize it couldn't buy him happiness. He had come to Arkansas looking for that happiness, for some greater purpose in life other than fame and fortune.

"He worked this farm for the love of the land," Emma said, "and because that's all Levi knew how to do. He didn't do it for the money; no farmer does." She took a deep breath and added defensively, "Levi had a metal box up in his bedroom where he had been saving extra cash in case of an emergency. The money went for medicine and doctors. I sold a load of chickens earlier than I normally would have to pay for his funeral expenses."

Brent snapped the journal closed. "I wasn't accusing you of anything, Emma."

"Everything's right there in black and white." She swept her arm in the direction of the desk. "I haven't had time lately to straighten the desk, but if you look you'll find seven years' worth of journals, accurate accounting on the chickens, tax receipts, and just about everything else." Her hands jammed onto her hips and she glared at him. "There is no money here, Haywood. Never has been, never will be."

"I'm not looking for money!" How could she possibly think he was after money? He had enough money stashed away to buy this farm a couple times over, and that didn't include the trust fund his father had set up for him when his parents split up.

"Then you are looking to sell?"

He noticed the hopeful note in her voice, and immediately squashed it. "I'm not selling." He didn't know what he was looking to do, but selling his share of the farm wasn't in his plans, at least not yet. He had come there to think, to plan his future, and hopefully connect somehow with a grandfather he had barely known. This farm was the closest thing he had to roots. His mother was constantly in transit from one high society hot spot to another, and changing husbands about as often. At last report she was separated from number five, but knowing his mother, she was either married to a number six already or reconciling with number five. He had moved around so much as a boy, he had been thankful when he'd finally entered an expensive prep school in upstate New York. At least nine months out of the year he had the same bedroom.

"You aren't planning on living here, are you?" Emma asked.

"Why not?"

A colorful curse tumbled from her mouth. "You can't be serious! There's nothing here but heat, hard work, and senseless chickens."

Brent blanched at the hard curse that had emerged from her delicate looking throat. "Where did you learn to swear like that?" he demanded.

"My father taught me that one." She angled her chin up in the air. "He didn't cotton to nursery rhymes, and the only time he used the word *mother*, it didn't precede *goose.*"

Brent studied the resentful look darkening her face and sadly shook his head. Could a father really have talked so foully in front of his daughter? "He sounds like a charming man."

"That's my dear old dad, oozing the charm, all right." Emma walked back into the kitchen and filled the sink with warm soapy water. "I'll do the dishes tonight; you can take your turn tomorrow night."

Brent could tell she expected an argument from him. He wasn't about to give her one. "Sounds fair to me." He carefully poured his hot chili from the pan into a bowl.

She cocked one eyebrow in response before walking into the mudroom. She pulled the wet jeans from the washer and dropped them into an old wicker laundry basket that looked as though it had been run over by a tractor.

Brent sat down at the table and watched as she stuffed a bunch of T-shirts, bras, and undies into the washer. Mrs. Butterfield, his mother's house-keeper, would have had a stroke at the way Emma loaded a washer. He could still picture the small piles of laundry spread across the laundry room floor every Monday morning. Darks, reds, towels, sheets, colors, and whites each had their own separate pile. All of his mother's unmentionables were placed by the laundry tub so Mrs. Butterfield could hand wash each piece. Nothing had ever been jammed into a washer. During his childhood he had worshiped the ground Mrs. Butterfield walked on. Not only was she his mother figure, his father figure, and the housekeeper rolled into one, she was his friend. When a problem arose, she was the one he went to for advice.

He finished the rubbery-tasting chili and followed Emma out the back door. She was standing in the light that spilled from the mudroom windows as she hung the load of jeans. "Do you always hang laundry at night?"

"Only when I want to wear clean jeans the next day."

"But it's dark, how do you expect them to dry?"

"Wet clothes don't care if it's day or night, only that it's dry." She clipped another pair to the line. "And any fool can see that it's so dry out, a person could spit and it would evaporate before it hit the ground."

Brent sighed and rubbed the back of his neck. "Is there any particular reason why you don't like me, or are you this cranky with everyone?"

Emma had just finished hanging the last pair of jeans. She spun around and stared at him in shock. *"Cranky?"*

He instinctively took a step backward. She looked mad enough to pull out the butcher knife she carried in her back pocket. He flashed her his winning smile, the one the advertising executives swore made every female under the age of seventy swoon. "Maybe *cranky* was the wrong word." *Hostile* had a better ring to it, but he wasn't about to tell her that. He wasn't sure what he was going to do with his life, but if he ever needed to get back into modeling, it would be a heck of a lot easier without scars. "You seem a little on edge since I arrived."

"Let me set you straight, city boy," she growled. "You show up here expecting Lord only knows what. You don't like the food, you don't like the way I do my laundry, and you practically accuse me of stealing from Levi."

"I did no such—"

"I'm not finished yet!" she shouted. She straightened her back and somehow managed to glare down at him. Considering he was six foot three, and he guessed she barely topped five foot six, it was no easy feat. "I've been up since four o'clock this morning plowing fields, taking care of chickens, and fixing the stuck carburetor on the truck. You just witnessed the only break I had in sixteen hours. I'm hot, tired, and in desperate need of a cool shower. If I want to act *cranky* in my own home, that is my God-given right, and if you don't like it, go to your half of the house and @&*@."

The rest of the sentence caused a tide of red to sweep up Brent's face. "If you don't stop using that word, I'll . . ."

"You'll what?" she taunted as she stalked back into the mudroom.

"I'll wash your mouth out with soap," he snapped as he followed her. It was the only thing he could think of to say. Mrs. Butterfield had threatened the bar-of-soap routine with him the one and only time he had used profanity within her earshot.

Emma's mouth fell open, then her boisterous laughter filled the mudroom and spilled over into the night. "Old Levi must surely be turning in his grave."

"Why?"

"To think his one and only grandson is such an innocent that he turns all pink in the face at a simple four-letter word. I wonder what you're going to do when you see me really get upset about something."

"I'll probably take you over my knee and teach you some manners." He didn't like being called innocent or the fact that Emma had spotted his slight flush. He had heard plenty of curses in his life, and no one could walk into a public bathroom without seeing smut written all over the walls. But it didn't mean such language was a mainstay of his vocabulary. What kind of life did Emma live that she used words like that as easily as she said her own name?

"If you lay one hand on me, I will guarantee you one thing." She slipped her hand into her back pocket. "No one will ever call you pretty boy again."

Brent's gaze followed the movement of her hand. Her message was loud and clear. Emma Carson was a fighter. He noted her rigid stance, her wide-eyed glare. She was putting on a brave front, but he could detect the fear behind the facade. Something in life had forced Emma to be a fighter. The need to comfort her was powerful, but he resisted, knowing how she'd react. "I won't lay one hand on you, Emma." His gaze locked on her moist mouth, and he wondered what she would taste like. Against his own judgment he softly added, "Unless you want me to."

"You expect me to want you to beat me?"

"That wasn't what I was referring to, and you know it." His meaning had been perfectly clear to her. He had noticed the way her eyes widened for the briefest of seconds, and how her gaze had shifted to his mouth.

"It had better be what you were referring to, Haywood." An unfriendly gleam glazed over her eyes. "If you try any funny business, your poor old mama won't ever hold a grandchild." She stared at his crotch while patting her back pocket. "Get my drift?"

"You're a hard woman, Emma." He uncomfortably shifted his weight, but one side of his mouth was lifting in a smile.

"The name's Carson." She glanced at the washer and headed back into the kitchen. "I'm taking a shower, and the only reason I'm telling you is because the door doesn't lock and I wouldn't want you accidentally walking in and having the misfortune of encountering a sharp instrument and ending the family bloodline."

Brent chuckled as she stormed out of view. He liked Emma, liked her spunk. There wasn't a woman known to him who could have handled this situation with such aplomb. The women from his world wouldn't dream of sharing a house with a total stranger. They were taught since childhood to lock their doors, not to talk to strangers, and to always, no matter what, act like a lady. Emma had broken every one of those rules within an hour and a half of meeting him.

Strawberry Ridge, Arkansas, was a long way from New York City, and not just in miles. Still, Brent locked the back door. Old habits die hard.

Emma stood under the shower and allowed the cool water to wash away the dirt and sweat. She wished the water could wash away her doubts too. For the past couple of weeks she had given a great deal of thought to what she would do when Levi's grandson finally showed up to claim his half of the inheritance. After a lot of number crunching and thinking, she was positive the bank would loan her the money to buy Brent out if she put her half of the farm up for collateral. It was a risky venture on her part. She was barely making ends meet now, but if she built a few more chicken enclosures and doubled the size of her poultry business, she just might be able to keep her head above water. There wasn't enough acreage to make a sizable income in corn; besides, a drought or flood could wipe her out totally if she relied on farming. By doubling the size of her chicken operation, she could manage, providing one of the dozen or so diseases known to infect chickens didn't wipe her out. It was a hell of a decision, but she didn't see any other options. She wanted to build the Amazing Grace Farm into the best free-range chicken farm in Arkansas.

She picked up the bottle of shampoo and started to wash one of her vanities, her hair. Long hair was impractical, considering her profession, but she kept it anyway. It was hot and heavy during the summer months, the amount of shampoo and conditioner required was expensive, and if she didn't keep it braided and tucked under a hat, it was constantly in her way. Still, she had never given in to the million or so urges to cut it. Every time she looked into the mirror and saw the nearly waist-length golden hair, she was reminded that underneath her T-shirts, flannel shirts, and rough jeans, she was a woman. She'd be the first one to admit that over the years, she had become quite adept at hiding that fact.

When she bought clothes, she purchased work jeans geared toward teenage boys, because they ran about twenty bucks cheaper than the fancy faded designer jeans for women. She never could see the sense in buying flowery pink T-shirts for ten bucks a pop, when she could walk over to the men's department and pick up pocket T-shirts on sale for about four dollars. Call her an idiot, but she would rather spend thirty dollars on three heavy flannel shirts than on one silk blouse she had absolutely nowhere to wear. Still, just because she dressed both sensibly and economically didn't mean she wasn't one hundred percent female. And her second vanity proved it. Her top drawer was fairly bursting with silken undies in every conceivable color.

She frowned as she rinsed out the shampoo and squirted on conditioner. She had made a fool of herself with Haywood by threatening him with a knife if he went peeking where he shouldn't. The day a man as gorgeous as Brent Haywood wanted to peek in on her was the day she would have to check her skin to make sure it hadn't turned green with purple polka dots. He sure as hell wasn't going to be looking at her just because she was female. Haywood must have plenty of girlfriends, oodles of them. Hell, he might even have a wife somewhere, or a fiancée. Men who looked liked Haywood didn't sit at home on Saturday nights watching "disease of the month" movies on an old television. They also weren't interested in women like her. Her brothers had told her men liked three things in a woman: large breasts, empty heads, and a mouth that only said "yes." Emma's one and only experience with a man, or to be more accurate, a boy, had proven her brothers right.

She stepped out of the shower, quickly dried off, and pulled on a T-shirt and a pair of boxer shorts with a crazy cartoon cat printed all over them. It was her summer sleepwear, cool and comfortable. She wrapped her hair in a towel and left the bathroom. There was an old robe hanging on the back of the door, and with a muttered curse she put it on. She was no longer alone in the house. Having Haywood there was becoming more of a nuisance than she had thought it would be. The sun had gone down, and the temperature had dropped into the low eighties, but the house was still holding the heat. Air-conditioning was a luxury Levi had never considered. The first summer Emma worked there, she'd had to go out and buy her own fan for her room. She counted her blessings that every room had at least one window with a screen in it.

At the bottom of the stairs she saw Brent squatting in front of the television in the living room, fiddling with the controls. He appeared to be trying to get a better picture. "That's the best it receives," she said.

"You're kidding." He glanced away from the fuzzy screen and over at her. His mouth seemed to drop to his knees before he snapped it shut.

She didn't like his stunned expression. The shower, she knew, hadn't improved her appearance that much. She had only been dusty and sweaty. He should see her when it poured rain for days and she had to wallow around in mud up to her knees. Then a shower could make a world of difference. The nicest thing she could say about the faded blue robe was that it was threadbare—therefore, cool—and ended at mid-thigh, so her legs weren't sweltering in its depths. "The antenna blew over about two months ago, and I haven't had time to straighten it out."

"Antenna? Don't you have cable?"

She chuckled and shook her head. "Cable? Where do you think you are, Little Rock? You have a choice of three channels that come in fuzzy and one channel that is hazy, but the voices are clear." She continued on her way to the mudroom and a washer full of wet laundry that needed to be hung before she could finally fall asleep.

Brent followed her. "What do you do for entertainment around here?"

"Entertainment?" Her eyes grew wide with amazement. "It's almost ten o'clock and I have to be up by four." She started to unload the washer.

"There's no VCR or CD player?"

"Listen, Haywood. Here's a simple rule for you. If it has initials, it's not here." She marched out back and started to pin the laundry to the line. Brent had the same expression someone would wear if he were transported back into the Stone Age. The look on his face should have been comical, but it wasn't. Several months back she had finally saved enough to buy a VCR, but the money had gone for medicine for Levi. He had needed the painkillers more than she'd needed to see Mel Gibson strut his stuff across the TV screen.

Brent stood in the mudroom and watched as Emma angrily clipped a rainbow of silky panties to the line. He had given those colorful panties a great deal of thought while she was upstairs in the shower. They were a contradiction. Everything about Emma was an inconsistency. The woman he had met in the barn and shared a canned dinner with had been rough and hard-edged. She had a mouth like a sailor, threatened him with a knife, and dressed like a man. She also had the strength to run this farm single-handed, and had taken care of a dying man for months. Emma had loved Levi, not as a woman loves a man, but as a friend.

She alone had been there when Levi needed someone. Brent cursed his mother and her selfish ways once again. It wasn't until Levi's lawyer had finally tracked him down, weeks after Levi's death, that he had even known his grandfather had been sick, let alone had died. When he had confronted his mother, she had admitted to receiving two telephone calls from some woman regarding Levi. She had ignored both messages, figuring that if her father needed something that badly, he would call himself. Emma had tried to contact Levi's family, only to be ignored.

He shuddered at what Emma must be thinking about him. And she was right. Ignorance was no excuse. He should have been checking in with his grandfather over the years and making sure he had everything he needed, instead of fluttering from one shoot to another. Family ties were one thing in life he had never experienced, and it appeared he had blown his only chance at them.

His father had agreed to a huge settlement with his mother and an impressive amount of money in trust for him from the divorce proceedings. There had been no visitation rights and no further contact because that was how his father had wanted it. A clean break for his father, and a confused two-year-old boy who didn't understand what had transpired. His mother had always treated him like a friend instead of a son. She did it more to conceal her true age than as a true sense of comradeship. Now, with his grandfather's death, he discovered there was a huge hole in his heart where a family should have been.

He continued to watch Emma as she hung T-shirts and bras on the line. She may or may not be the real Emma, he mused. She looked adorable dressed in that frumpy old robe with her hair wrapped in a beige bath towel piled high on her head, giving him an enticing glimpse of her graceful neck. He had no idea what she had on under the robe, but he prayed it was something hideous. His imagination could only stand so much pressure, and the length of her long, stunning legs had already caused it to go into overdrive. When she had walked into the living room and he had first glimpsed those remarkable legs, his heart had stopped pumping and every ounce of blood had rushed to a very sensitive part of his body. He didn't want to think about Emma like that. She was his partner and they were going to have to share this cramped little house for a while. It was going to get awfully embarrassing for him if he continued to react to her like this.

His gaze followed her legs upward until the frayed hem of the robe obscured his view about mid-thigh. He knew her hips were well rounded and her waist narrow, because he had seen her in tight jeans earlier. Her breasts had been on the lush side, but firm, as the moist T-shirt had clung to them. His gaze rose higher, caressing her throat and face. With her hair pulled up and away from her face, her features were more pronounced.

Brent silently groaned as heat ignited deep in his gut. He was in trouble, deep trouble. His little hoyden of a partner had the profile of an angel against the night's darkness.

THREE

Emma saw Brent coming, but grabbed the half-empty bag of feed and made her way into the chicken run. Sleepyhead had finally awakened, and it was barely seven o'clock. Considering the amount of work he had done the night before, the man must not have hit the bed much before three. She hadn't been surprised when he hadn't joined her for coffee and cereal; not many people willingly left their beds at four-thirty. But she had been taken aback by the clean desk in the living room. Brent must have spent most of the night straightening papers, filing, and acquainting himself with the business end of the Amazing Grace Farm while she had slept.

As she carefully measured out the feed, she wondered if he was now ready to sell. The books didn't lie. There wasn't an extra penny anywhere.

"'Mornin', partner." Brent flashed her his pearly whites. "Sorry about oversleeping."

She glanced up from the feeder and the dozen or so chickens hungrily pecking at the fresh food. "Didn't much expect to see a city boy like you before lunchtime."

"The name's Brent," he said, sounding as if his teeth were clenched. "Aren't you going to invite me in and introduce me to our bread-and-butter?"

She purposely stared at his immaculately clean and brilliant white sneakers. She had seen those same shoes advertised once in the Sunday paper. For the price he had paid for them, she could have bought Roscoe's beat-up old pickup truck complete with a full tank of gas. "If you step in here you'll get those fancy sneakers covered with chicken *&$@."

Brent opened the wired door and stepped inside. "They'll wash." He glanced at the ground and the nervously squawking birds backing away from him. "Couldn't you have called it something else?"

"Chicken poo-poo?" She grinned. She doubted that she had used the word *poo-poo* even when she was being potty-trained. Her father was a strict believer in calling things what they were. Emma had no memories of her mother, but her brothers had told her that she used to give cutesy names to everything, making their father furious. Emma never gave anything a cutesy name because she knew her father's temper and had learned early in life to fear it.

"*Chicken droppings* would have done nicely." Brent surveyed the noisy chickens. "How come these guys are still in their pen when the pen closest to the house is empty and there're dozens of chickens strutting around the backyard?"

"Right now there are four chicken runs. Every morning I alternate opening one and allowing the chickens to roam free for the day."

"Why only one?"

"Because if I open all four, they'll get all mixed up, and each run has a different age chicken. Besides, rounding up over a hundred birds and shooing them back into the run is bad enough. If I had over five hundred to do each night, I'd never get to bed."

"You have five hundred chickens?"

"No, *we* have approximately seven hundred and fifty chickens, sixty brooding hens, nine roosters, and as of this morning around two hundred and ten eggs being sat upon."

"That's a lot of chickens."

"Tomorrow the figure drops by about one hundred and twenty-five."

"Why?"

"Remember that group you saw scratching up the backyard?"

"Yes."

"Tomorrow they get shipped off to the packers." Emma retied the bag of feed and carried it to the truck. She filled two buckets of water from the tank in the bed.

"Packers?" Brent had followed her out of the run and automatically picked up the two buckets. A slight grunt was the only indication of their weight.

Emma opened the gate and made sure none of the birds escaped for greener grass and juicy worms. "Meat packers, Haywood." She shook her head as his mouth fell open. "What did you think we were raising them for? Farm shows?" She took one of the buckets and dumped it into the trough. Brent dumped the other one.

"I knew they were being raised for food," he said. "It's just that I've never raised or met my own dinner before."

"Don't worry, you won't be eating any chicken here. I'm so sick of hearing and looking at chickens by the end of the day that if someone tried to feed me one, I would end up choking." She started to circle the run, glancing at the ground and the chickens.

Brent followed her gaze and stayed right behind her. "What are we looking for?"

Emma felt the first crack in the wall she had built around her heart. He seemed so sincere and willing to help. "I don't know what you're looking for, but I'm examining the outer walls for signs of animals trying to burrow their way in. I'm also checking out the chickens to make sure there aren't any signs of diseased or sickly ones."

"What kind of animals want to come in?"

"Foxes mainly." She walked around the large wooden coop built at the far end of the run and

cautiously glanced inside. The smell nearly
knocked her over. Tomorrow, if she had time, she
needed to change the straw lying on the coop's
floor. This group of chickens still had another two
or three weeks to go before becoming someone's
dinner. With the intense heat they had been experiencing lately, the smell of chicken droppings was a
little more pronounced than usual. "Then there are
also the rats and the occasional weasel and mink."

"Sounds charming." He studied the ground
around the outer wall more closely. "I didn't know
rats ate chickens."

"They don't, but they will eat their feed and
any eggs they can get their little claws on."

"I gather the eggs and little ones are kept in the
two buildings by the barn."

Emma glanced at him, momentarily thrown off
balance by his obvious interest. She had expected
him to be announcing that he was heading back to
New York. Especially after seeing all the books.
Breaking even was a luxury in the history of the
Amazing Grace Farm. Most years began in the red
and ended in the red. She couldn't think of one
good reason why he wanted to stay. "If you're
really that interested in the farm, I'll give you a tour
later." Maybe after he had the nickel tour of the
place, his curiosity would be satisfied and he would
leave her in peace to run the farm. She wasn't worried about doing all the work and then having to
share the profits with him. There weren't any profits.

"How about if I follow you around for the next couple of days and you can explain as we go? That way I could start taking over some of the work and pulling my share."

Emma didn't like the sound of that. "How long are you planning on staying here?"

"I haven't decided yet."

"Don't you have a job to get back to?" What was this? An Arkansas rendition of *City Slickers?*

"I gave up my job and I subleased my apartment." He looked down the slight hill at the weather-beaten house below. "Amazing Grace is now my home."

Emma muttered a word that had gotten her three days' suspension from school back in the seventh grade. "Are you hiding from a wife and a bunch of kiddies?"

"I'm not, nor have I ever been married." He scowled at her. "What did I tell you about using such language?"

She ignored the comment on her language; she had heard it all before. "Isn't there a fiancée, a girlfriend, or someone who is going to miss you?"

"I have friends whom I will miss, but no one important person as you're referring to."

"What about your mother?" Over the years, she had observed that most people had strong family ties, and around Strawberry Ridge folks tended to stick close by one another. Hell, she had heard stories that up in the more isolated regions of the Ozarks, they even married within their own family.

The Carson family was the exception. It had been months since she'd seen her father, and then it had been only by accident, bumping into him while in town.

"My mother and I don't have the typical mother-son relationship," Brent replied.

She wondered what in the hell that meant. It looked like she was going to be stuck with Pretty Boy until he got sick of hauling feed and water to a bunch of witless creatures. Then again, maybe it would only take shoveling out poo-poo-crusted straw from some cramped chicken coop to make him strut his stuff back to New York.

"If you want to spend your time developing blisters on those baby-smooth palms, fine by me. I could use the extra time to do about a hundred other things around here." She left the run with Haywood right behind her. She double-checked to make sure the gate was properly closed. "I have one more run to take care of, then it's on to the nesting building and then the nursery." She climbed in the old pickup and fired up the engine while Haywood plopped his gorgeous tush down on the ripped vinyl seat next to her.

Brent was enthralled by the sight before him. For the past hour he had been leaning against one of the main support poles in the nesting building and watching a clutch of eggs hatch. Earlier that morning Emma had pointed out the cracked eggs and the faint little cheeping coming from inside. She explained how the chicks were in the process of hatching and that it could take up to fourteen hours for the entire clutch of eight chicks to hatch. After fixing some peanut butter and jelly sandwiches for lunch, and making sure Emma ate, he had driven into town and spent a small fortune in the one and only grocery store. He had also stopped at a store and picked up some work clothes and a pair of sturdy boots. Emma had been right. His sneakers would never be the same again.

After putting a roast in the oven, he'd come out to the nesting building to check on the eggs. Emma had also been right about the chicks taking so long. Only two fuzzy yellow chicks were nestled under their mother's wing, and one other wet, limp chick had finally managed to break free of the shell. The other five eggs were in various stages of hatching. He had never witnessed anything more breathtakingly wonderful than these little fellows struggling for life. With each cracked piece of egg breaking off, he felt a jolt of something that felt suspiciously like pride.

He knew it was a senseless feeling; he was neither the father nor responsible for the mother hen's health. Emma had seen to that singlehandedly. He had been in awe during the entire tour around the chicken runs and the two buildings where it all began. He had never imagined the work and care that were required to raise a chicken. The runs were for protection against the chickens' natural enemies and a way to keep them together, but still allow them plenty of freedom to roam, scratch for food, and dust bathe. The wooden coops built into the runs provided a safe place for them to rest at night, keep warm and dry, and perch. The three days the chickens were in the run, Emma supplemented their diet of worms, seeds, grains, and other insects, with a specially formulated feed and plenty of fresh, clean water.

Emma had thought of everything and did everything, from start to finish. He had never met a woman like her before in his life. His women friends in New York tended to be in the same profession as his, modeling. They also tended to be slightly self-absorbed. Worrying about crow's-feet, an extra two pounds, and who got on what cover were all major concerns. Emma didn't seem to have a self-absorbed bone in her body.

He sighed as a tiny piece of shell broke away from one of the eggs. It was the only egg that had shown no signs of hatching. He had begun to worry about the little fellow inside. Brent knew enough not to help the chick, but he had begun to feel compelled just to crack the shell and give the little guy a head start.

"So this is where you've been hiding," Emma said as she stepped inside the building and closed the door behind her.

Brent grinned at the picture she made in a bright pink T-shirt, jeans, and a white baseball cap with her thick golden braid hanging down her back.

She looked hot and tired and amazingly sexy. Here was a woman who would look beneath the exterior to find the man. "Is the planting done?"

"Yes." She glanced over at the hen and the three baby chicks huddling under her wing. "They appear to be healthy."

"Oh, they are." Brent pointed to the latest chick that had emerged. "See that little fellow? He's drying off nicely, and the other five eggs are getting there. That one is just about out, and this one just started to crack. I was beginning to worry about that one, but it appears okay now." He leaned in closer and smiled fondly at the eggs.

Emma nervously shifted her feet. "Ah, Brent."

He snapped his head around at the use of his first name. Emma had an annoying habit of calling him Haywood, pretty boy, or city boy, never his first name. His gut reaction was telling him something was wrong. He glanced back at the eggs. They all appeared to be progressing nicely, but what did he know about chicks? "What's wrong?" he demanded.

"How long have you been here watching the eggs?"

"About an hour, why?"

She sighed and shook her head. "I think you're becoming too personally involved."

"With who?"

"The chicks." She stretched out a finger and stroked the top of one of the chicks' head. Mama hen clucked nervously until Emma backed away. "I

realize they are cute, adorable, and fuzzy little crit-
ters who could worm their way straight into an un-
suspecting heart the minute they emerge from the
egg." She looked away from the peeping chicks to
Brent. "But you must realize that tomorrow they
get moved over to the nursery until they're four
weeks old, and then it's out to the runs."

Brent didn't need her to say the rest. He knew
they would stay in the runs until they were about
fifteen weeks old, then it was off to the packers.
"How do you stay so detached?"

She glanced at the row of nesting boxes, each
containing a brooding hen and her eggs. "Who
says I do?" She purposely walked to the door and
opened it. Afternoon sunlight streamed in, causing
a ruckus of clucking from the hens. "Come on outside and I'll give you your first driving lesson on a
tractor."

Brent hesitated for a second before following
her out into the daylight. He had seen a veil of
something soft and loving drop over Emma's features as she tenderly stroked the chick. She wasn't
immune to the wonder of it all. She had been no
more detached than he was. She only hid it better.

Emma glanced up from her second helping of
the tenderest roast beef she had ever tasted. "Why
didn't you tell me you can cook? I never would
have shown you how to drive the tractor if I knew."

"What does cooking a simple roast have to do with my driving the tractor?"

"You probably will want to spend your days turning up fields instead of cooking dinner." There was nothing *simple* about the roast, she thought, or anything concerning Brent Haywood. The man could rival Mel Gibson in a battle of looks, outcook Chef Boyardee, and he did laundry to boot. The load of towels that had been lying on the mudroom floor the night before were now washed, dried, and neatly folded. So were the rest of her jeans, shirts, and undergarments. She'd never had anyone do her laundry before, and she didn't like the uncomfortable feeling it gave her. Brent had taken time out of his day to stand in the mudroom and fold all her panties neatly in half. It had too much of an intimate feeling about it, but she'd be damned if she knew how to broach the subject with him. Since she'd been big enough to stand on a stool in the backyard and reach the clothesline, she had done her father's and all three of her older brothers' laundry. She had folded more men's and boys' underwear than she cared to remember and it had never once bothered her. Most of the time she had done Levi's laundry along with her own too. She used to offer laundry services for the week if he'd make up a large pot of his chili or his Gator Gut Stew. The stew didn't contain any alligator meat, and old Levi never did tell her the ingredients, but it had been delicious.

"Since you made dinner," she said, "I'll clean up tonight."

"I thought it was my turn."

"That was before I knew you could cook." She took the last biscuit and soaked up the gravy left on her plate. She couldn't remember the last time she'd had such a great meal. Once a month, usually on payday, she'd head into town, pick up whatever she needed, and stop in at Jake's Diner for a good home-cooked meal. She hadn't been to Jake's since before Levi took to his bed.

"Can't you cook?" Brent asked.

"So-so," she admitted. As she'd grown up and learned to cook, her successes had been met with demands for more, not with praise; and her failures, which were numerous, had been met with her father's anger.

"I bought a cake for dessert." Brent stood and started to remove the empty dishes. "Maybe after the kitchen is cleaned up we could sit down and have a discussion over coffee and cake."

"What kind of discussion?" she asked suspiciously. She knew it. Everything was going too smoothly with Brent.

"About the farm." He searched a cabinet until he found a bowl large enough to hold the leftover roast and potatoes.

"What about the farm?"

"Later, Emma." He sealed the bowl with wrap and placed it in the now full refrigerator. "How about if you wash and I'll dry?"

"How about if I wash and dry while you round up all the chickens in the backyard and make sure they get back to their run nice and safe before it gets dark." It was a rotten trick to pull on him, especially his first full day on the farm, but it had hurt that he wouldn't discuss whatever was on his mind now. The farm might only be half hers, but it was all she had. If he wanted to sell, she needed to know immediately so that she could start making arrangements with the bank. She suppressed a smile as Brent walked through the mudroom and out into the backyard.

An hour later a hassled looking Brent stood in the doorway of the mudroom glaring at Emma. "Wipe your feet," she called as she carried a tray containing their coffee and cake into the living room. "I just washed the kitchen floor, so be careful. It still might be damp." After she had washed and dried the dishes, she'd started feeling guilty for sending Brent out there alone to round up the chickens. So she'd washed the floor.

She should have at least given him some hints on how to do it. The two times she had glanced out the window, it had taken all her willpower to smother her laughter. The first time, Brent had been standing at one end of the yard nearest the run. He had whistled loudly and clapped his hands, trying to gain the birds' attention. He got it, all right. The entire hundred and twenty-two birds had run in the opposite direction, away from the noise. Later, when she'd looked out again, Brent was at the other end of the yard waving his arms wildly and shouting. All the chickens took off running in the direction of the enclosure. The only problem was, Brent hadn't opened the door first and the birds, not knowing what was happening, couldn't get into the run. They'd ended up going in every direction, except where Brent wanted them. After that, she couldn't bear to look, so she'd scrubbed the floor.

"You could have at least told me to open the run's door before I tried shooing them in that direction." Brent kicked off his dusty boots before walking across the kitchen floor.

"You could have asked." Her smile was pure innocence as she sat down in an old rocking chair. When she was nervous, she needed to keep moving. Rocking would help conceal that fact from Brent. She waved an arm in the direction of the couch. "Sit and start talking."

He sat down and leaned his head back. "You don't waste time, do you?"

"Don't see the sense in wasting something I have so little of."

"Hmmm . . ." He took a sip of coffee. "As you may have already guessed, I spent last night going over the books."

"Find anything interesting?" She knew what was there. Low income, heavy debts, and absolutely no profit.

"As a matter of fact, I did. It appears to me that the poultry end of the farm is what's keeping the bills paid."

Anyone who could balance a checkbook could have figured that out. "Let me guess, you were an accountant before you gave it all up for half ownership in a run-down chicken farm in Arkansas?"

"Did anyone ever tell you, you have a smart mouth?"

"Let me see." She started to tick off on her fingers. "First there was my kindergarten teacher. And then my first grade teacher, then my second grade teacher, and then—"

"I get the picture," Brent snapped.

Emma couldn't help it. Her smile turned into a full-fledged grin. She wasn't very happy about her smart mouth; it was one of the things she had been working on for years. Here she'd thought she had it under control, and she had, until Brent showed up. Levi had even joked occasionally about how she was such a docile little lamb compared to the wildcat she had been, fresh out of high school and her father's house, when he first hired her. He had even mentioned that he wouldn't have hired her as she was now, because she didn't act as if she had the guts or the ambition to run a farm. Back when she was eighteen, she would have taken on any job as long as it got her away from her father and her brothers. Eighteen years was a hell of a long time to live in their shadows. Freedom hadn't been everything she thought it would be, but she didn't mind. She had her independence. She took grief off of no one, including Levi, and he had respected that, even when he was ranting and raving about it. Emma wasn't about to let Pretty Boy Haywood start calling the shots. Her first defense was to try to intimidate him with her mouth. It seemed to be working.

"You enjoy doing that, don't you?" he said.

"What?" she asked innocently.

"Making people mad."

Her smile faded completely. His remark had scored a perfect bull's-eye. The more she liked a person, the more she gave flip answers, insults, and just plain old smart comments. It was a purely defensive maneuver. Attack first and push a person away before he or she could hurt you. Emma's defenses were on full alert where Brent was concerned. The more sides of himself he showed, the more she was beginning to like him, and that scared the hell out of her. Brent Haywood wasn't there to stay. In the long run he wouldn't want any part of her, the farm, or the handful of children she had always dreamed about.

Emma focused on her coffee cup and fortified the wall surrounding her heart. "I thought you wanted to talk about the farm, not me."

Brent studied her for a full minute before sighing. "I think I know how to make this farm more profitable, and still easily managed by just the two of us."

She raised an eyebrow and purred, "Do tell."

He ignored her tone and continued. "First thing we have to do is add another six, maybe even eight runs. The forty acres of corn is peanuts compared to what we could be pulling in if we had that land converted into more runs for chickens. We should continue to grow the hay in the remaining acres because we'll need it for the coops and henhouse. We also need a better system of delivering water and feed to the runs. Carrying all those buckets will get old fast."

Emma felt her ears burn and her hands tremble. How dare he waltz in here and in one day announce they needed to increase the poultry end of the farm? That had been her intention all along. She knew exactly what the farm needed; only problem was she needed a good twenty thousand dollars to start to make the essential changes. She pointed a shaking finger at Brent and growled, "Don't move."

She marched upstairs, threw open her bedroom door, and disappeared inside. Within seconds she was marching back down the stairs. With a violent thrust she shoved a notebook into Brent's hands. "Read it and weep."

Brent glanced down at the book. He studied the first page, then the second. By the time he was finished looking at all six pages, he understood Emma's anger. The notebook contained drawings and financial estimates for every detail he had just described, and a lot more he hadn't thought of.

Emma knew exactly what the farm needed. "I think I just stuck my foot in my mouth."

"How does it taste?"

He gave her his best smile. "Like I've been walking in chicken droppings all day." He flipped through the book again. He had to hand it to her, everything looked professional and well thought out. "Can I at least ask why you never implemented any of these changes?"

"Check out the last page." She waited until he turned to that page. "See the final figure?"

He glanced at it. It looked perfectly reasonable to him. The Amazing Grace Farm could make that back in three years, and from then on out it would be pure profit. "What about it?"

"Well, where do you expect it to come from, my &%#?"

"As charming a picture as that conjures up, I asked you very nicely to curb that mouth of yours."

Emma stood less than three feet away, glaring at him. "What are you going to do if I don't?"

Brent shoved a hand through his hair, disheveling it. Emma was driving him crazy. In twenty-four hours he had ping-ponged back and forth between the longing to turn her over his knee and the desire to kiss away the memory of every four-letter word she knew. The threat of washing her mouth out with soap hadn't fazed her, so maybe it was time to change tactics. "The next four-letter word that comes out of your mouth"—he dropped the notebook to the couch and glared right back at her—

"I'm going to kiss you until you have completely forgotten it."

The curse that slipped from Emma's mouth was purely accidental, or so she told herself.

Brent reached out and hauled her against his chest. "That does it," he said, and his mouth swooped down onto hers with deadly accuracy.

FOUR

Emma ceased breathing and her eyes widened in shock as Brent's lips covered hers. It wasn't a demanding or punishing kiss as she'd expected. It started out stormy and quickly turned into a tempest of warm sensations and desires. Her eyes slowly closed and her arms encircled his neck as she let herself drop into the vortex.

Brent gentled his hold and pulled her closer. With a sweep of his tongue he parted her lips and deepened the kiss. His fingers shook as one hand gripped her hip and the other threaded its way against the back of her head and into the silken braid.

Emma could feel the warmth of his fingers against her scalp and through the rough denim covering her hips. Shock waves of heat rolled over highly electrified nerve endings, jolting her with his very touch. She responded with a moan of pleasure to the surge of passion assaulting her body. This was the kind of kiss she had been dreaming about her whole life! This was how a kiss should be. Consuming. She wanted to savor its taste, its texture, and to experience it totally. With a boldness inspired by newly awakened desire, she met the thrust of Brent's demanding tongue and engaged it in a fiery duel.

A heavy groan vibrated deep within his chest as she pressed herself closer and her soft breasts crushed against him. The hand clutching her hip moved to her bottom and cupped it, propelling her hips forward.

The feel of his heavy arousal straining the front of his jeans shattered the pleasurable sensations his kiss had caused. A cry of dismay was torn from her lips as she broke the kiss and tried to step away from Brent. His hands still held her in a lover's embrace, though. A veil of white fear and red rage descended upon her. She instinctively reached for her knife as she cried, "Let me go!"

Brent immediately released her and stepped back. Confusion clouded the flush of heated desire etched onto his face. His breath came in jerky gasps. "Emma?" He tentatively reached for her again.

"Don't!"

"Don't what?" He lowered his hand back to his side and studied her face.

"Don't touch me. Don't kiss me." She took another step back, moving closer to the stairs. "Don't *ever* come near me again."

After delivering that final statement, she fled up the stairs, dashed into her room, slammed the door, and promptly burst into tears. What had she done! Not only had she allowed Brent to kiss her, she had actually kissed him back. Oh, and what a kiss it had been! With one kiss he had thawed every frozen molecule of desire she had locked away in the barren Siberia of her body. Brent Haywood had made her yearn for something more, and that scared the hell out of her. She wasn't sure if she would ever be capable of giving or accepting anything more. For one brief moment she had wanted to follow the delicious path of temptation he was blazing, and the next she had felt the heavy thrust of his response against her abdomen and had known only fear.

It had been her experience that men did nothing but take. Her father had taken a child's love and used it against her. Her brothers had taken her time and her energy for their own advantage. And Jack Roddman had taken her innocence and her naive schoolgirl's crush and shattered them in the front seat of his pickup.

Emma swiped at the tears rolling down her cheeks, bit her trembling lip, and willed the crying to stop. Brent was the wrong man to pin any hopes on. He wouldn't be staying long in Strawberry Ridge once he realized how hard, monotonous, and unrewarding raising chickens was. He was gorgeous, seemingly rich, and wore refinement the way she wore T-shirts. They couldn't have been more opposite if she had purposely tried. And no, she didn't believe opposites attracted. Evil generated evil, good produced good, and men like Brent weren't attracted to female chicken farmers from Arkansas.

He had kissed her either to shut her up or because she was the only eligible female within a five-mile radius. There was absolutely no other reason for his kiss—no matter what it had done to her body, or what her heart was crying out. He had a hard lesson to learn if he thought all he had to do was flash his sexy grin and she would fall to her knees and give him anything he wanted. For the last seven years she had stood up for herself and refused to be used by anyone for anything. Pretty Boy had better watch his p's and q's and where his kisses landed from now on, because she wasn't about to make the same mistake twice.

A wide grin spread across her face as she raised her fist to the closed door. "One wrong move, Haywood," she muttered, "and POW! right in the kisser." She chuckled as she snatched up her pajamas and headed for a cool shower and, if she was really lucky, six hours of sleep.

Brent was still standing at the bottom of the stairs when he heard Emma go into the bathroom, slamming the door behind her. Only two things registered in his mind. First, he had never before felt the instantaneous inferno of desire that had been ignited when he kissed Emma. He had kissed women before, plenty of women. Women he genuinely liked, women he was simply attracted to, and two women he'd thought he was falling in love with. But none of them had ever had this effect on him. The desire that had griped his gut when Emma's sweet mouth melted under his was enough to knock him to his knees.

The only thing preventing him from rushing up those stairs and picking up where they had left off was the fear he had seen in her eyes. Emma had been afraid either of him or of the billowing maelstrom their kiss had caused. The all too brief kiss had given him quite a jolt, and he considered himself jaded enough not to have been shocked by anything. He couldn't imagine what Emma must have felt.

A frown pulled at his brows as he continued to stand at the bottom of the stairs, gazing upward. What if Emma hadn't felt anything? That would only mean the fear that had been in her eyes was because of him, not their kiss. Why would she be afraid of him? He hadn't done anything to cause her to fear him.

He sat down on the bottom step and listened to the sound of the shower and the banging pipes. That morning when he had taken his shower, the sound of the clanking pipes had startled him at first, but then he'd picked up the rhythmic beat. By the time he was finished showering, he was singing an old Beatles song that blended in with the beat of the pipes. Tonight their clanking resembled something a heavy metal band would perform. He forced himself to concentrate on the clanging and not on the tempting picture that was forming in his head: Emma all naked and slick under the pounding spray, slowly rubbing every inch of her fabulous body with some slippery bar of soap.

With a muffled curse he stormed away from the stairs and marched into the kitchen. He was bone tired after the day he had put in, but he knew sleep would be a long time coming. Thanks to Emma. He never should have kissed her. How was he ever going to concentrate on the farm, finding his roots, or figuring out where his life was headed if all he thought about was the sweet taste of Emma's mouth?

He looked around the kitchen for something to do and came up empty. The place was fifty years out of date, but there was nothing he could do with it tonight. That afternoon when he'd unloaded the groceries, he had straightened out cabinets and acquainted himself with the rest of the room. Emma had washed and dried the dinner dishes, and even washed the floor.

Needing something to keep his hands and mind occupied, he hauled up two empty boxes from the basement and proceeded to fill them with the array of coats, boots, shoes, and assorted junk in the mudroom. He gutted the entire room, except for the washer and a can of sunflower yellow paint he had found under an inch of dust, and shoved the boxes out the back door. The mudroom was only six feet wide, but it ran the entire length of the kitchen, which was twelve feet. It shouldn't take him more than a couple of hours to brighten up one room of the house, and maybe it would tire him out enough so he could sleep without dreaming about his partner.

Three days later Emma was about ready to admit defeat. Defeat of what she wasn't sure, but she couldn't go on living this way. The guilt was eating her alive. Brent was running circles around her, and she could barely keep her eyes open. It wasn't helping matters that every time she lay down and closed her eyes, she relived their kiss. Or the fact that Brent was being polite, totally unthreatening, acting as if he'd invented the word *nice*. He never once mentioned the kiss. He joined her every morning in the kitchen for breakfast, and after three days of "showing him the ropes," she had enough confidence in his abilities to handle the chicken runs that she didn't watch his every move. The day before, he had even helped catch and cage over a hundred chickens for the packers without batting an eye. Afterward he had scrubbed down and disinfected the empty coop, a job she wouldn't wish on her worst enemy, for the next batch of chickens without a complaint. She still oversaw the nursery

and the nesting buildings, but Brent had shown remarkable insight, common sense, and interest in
those two areas, so she continued teaching him and
answering his questions. When he wasn't busy with
the chickens, he spent his time working on the
house, running errands into town, and generally
being so damn helpful she didn't know what to do.

Within the past couple of days he had painted
the mudroom yellow with dark green trim and had
hung curtains with huge sunflowers printed on
them across the back windows. Dark green rugs
covered the faded linoleum, windows sparkled in
the morning light, and all of Levi's old clutter had
been tossed. The room looked so good, she now
felt compelled to remove her dusty boots on the
back stoop before she walked in.

The kitchen had received the same treatment.
Fresh white paint had replaced the faded wallpaper,
crisp red-and-white-checked curtains brightened
the room, and a large braided rug woven with reds
and whites covered just about every inch of the
worn floor. The wooden cabinets gleamed, cute
magnets crowded the refrigerator door, and a huge
ceramic bowl sat in the middle of the table overflowing with fresh fruit. The dining room was in
the process of being redone. That morning over
breakfast Brent had asked her opinion on the paint.
He had one of his grandmother's good china plates
and was trying to match the flowers in its design.
She had no idea what had propelled her to tell him
she'd always pictured the room painted pale peach

with white lacy curtains. Immediately after he pulled that confession out of her, she had fled the house and hid in the barn for the rest of the morning on the pretense of tuning up the tractor.

The realization that Levi's old house was rapidly turning into a home had given her a jolt. The warm feeling that squeezed her heart every time she entered the house now was too damn comforting. She wasn't one hundred percent sure what was causing it, the bright, cheerful, relaxing rooms, or Brent. For the seven years she had lived there with Levi, she had never felt as if the house were her home. But then again she'd never felt that her father's run-down mobile home on a barren half acre on the outskirts of town was a home either. It had been more like a prison. Levi's house had been a safe place to lay her head at night after a hard day's work, and her room was a good spot to hold all her worldly possessions, which could have fit in a couple of large cardboard boxes. But it had never been a home to her.

Now she found herself enjoying a second cup of coffee in the cheerful kitchen, discussing the day's chores with Brent, while watching the sun rise. And the night before, she had taken a quiet half hour for herself to sit on the front porch and watch the sun set behind the mountains in the west. Brent had sat on the top step, within three feet of her, and not said a word until the fiery ball had disappeared. When he did speak, it was only to tell her he was starting in on the dining room. She'd been disappointed when he left, but she'd been more disappointed in herself for not starting a conversation with him that didn't include chickens, hay yields, or the farm. She wanted to know more about the man she was living with, like what he'd done for a living before coming to Arkansas. Tonight, she vowed, she would open her mouth and ask some questions.

Emma gently closed the hood on the old John Deere and gave the tractor a loving pat. The poor thing was probably in shock after all the work and new parts she had just given it. It wasn't used to anything being replaced before breaking down totally. The day before when Brent had returned from town carrying paint chips, more food, and air-conditioning brochures, he had presented Emma with a box full of new parts for the tractor. She had started to stammer out a thank you, but he'd brushed it aside, saying that without the tractor the farm was sunk. He knew she was worse than an old mother hen with the John Deere and had probably bought the parts to please her. Yet he'd refused a simple thank you. Well, two could play at that game, she thought.

She gave the tractor one last swipe of a rag across the hood and surveyed the junk lying around the huge barn. Two-by-fours were scattered here and there, two sheets of plywood in pretty good condition were buried under a small mountain of cobwebs, and partial rolls of chicken wire lay everywhere. It looked like she had everything she needed to start phase one of increasing the production of the Amazing Grace Farm.

Forty-five minutes later Brent found Emma in back of the barn surrounded by a pile of wood, saws, and assorted tools. How a woman wearing a man's T-shirt streaked in dust and grease could look so appealing was beyond him. Even when she was rumpled, sweaty, and dirty, Emma was still the most fascinating woman he had ever encountered. For the past three days he had been slowly going out of his mind thinking about her. He also had been working himself into a state of exhaustion every night just so he could catch a few hours of sleep without dreaming about her. The house had been the lucky recipient of all his excess energy. By the look of things, though, it was going to take another year of overabundant energy to get the place in shape, because Levi had lived by one rule—never throw anything away. Time was something Brent didn't have. He had already contacted the storage company where all his furniture from his apartment was stored and told them to deliver it to the farm. It seemed senseless to him to store top-quality furniture in a warehouse while living with a saggy mattress, and a couch with broken springs and stuffing escaping from a multitude of holes. All his belongings were due to arrive before the end of the month. Maybe he should prepare Emma.

He watched as she tried to hold two boards together and hammer a nail at the same time. She ended up hitting her thumb and cursing.

"What did I tell you about swearing?" He stepped out of the shadow of the barn and walked toward her.

She jerked around at the sound of his voice and released the boards she had been holding. Both of them landed on her left foot. "Dammit, Brent, don't sneak up on me like that!" She grabbed the toes of her left foot and jammed her thumb into her mouth while glaring at him. A second curse was muttered around the thumb.

Brent tenderly pulled her thumb out from between her lips and examined it. There was a big red spot where the hammer had connected with it, but he didn't think she'd broken anything. "That's two you owe me."

"Two what?"

"Kisses." His gaze never left the bruised, slightly moist thumb.

She jerked her hand away while maintaining her one-legged stance. "If you think I'm going to kiss you every time I feel like cussing, you're out of your mind."

He flashed her a grin. "Quite possibly." He glanced down at the foot she was still clutching. "How about if you take off your boot so I can see what damage you did to your foot?"

"How about if I take my boot and shove it—"

"Are you purposely trying for three?" He liked the idea of Emma actively seeking his kisses. The flush staining her cheeks could have been caused by desire, but he had a gut feeling it had more to do with anger.

"Listen, Haywood, I would rather swap spit with a copperhead than kiss you again."

Her eyes weren't shooting daggers; it looked more like that lethal looking knife she carried around in her back pocket. He decided to back off before he lost a vital part of his anatomy. "Calm down. I wasn't going to collect them right now. I'm going to allow you to start an I.O.U. system."

"Haywood!"

He decided he'd better drop it. The fiery red sweeping up her face was definitely not from desire. He glanced at the pile of wood and chicken wire. "What are you building?"

For a moment he didn't think she was going to respond. With a heavy sigh she said, "Another chicken run, I hope."

"Why *you hope?*"

"I might not have enough wire to make it as big as I would like."

"How big do you need it?" He glanced at the assorted rolls of wire and frowned. There appeared to be enough to cage in every chicken in Strawberry Ridge.

"*We* need it pretty big if *we* are going to increase the number of chickens *we* produce." She picked up the hammer from where she'd dropped it when she'd smacked her thumb. "We have to pick out some hens and a couple more roosters from our stock and raise them separately. A hen can't produce a fertile egg until she's fully mature, which usually takes about a year. So it's going to take till next spring before we see a dramatic increase in our stock."

"That should give us plenty of time to harvest the crops we have growing, build the runs, and fix this place up a little." He picked up the two boards she had been nailing, removed the hammer from her hand, and finished nailing them together.

"Aren't you forgetting one little detail?" she asked.

"What's that?"

"Money, moola, the twenty thousand green ones that I calculated we would need to even begin to increase our productivity. And that wasn't figuring anything for fixing this place up, as you so graciously put it."

Brent ignored the way her voice rose with each word. "I guess I forgot to mention the loan."

"What loan?"

"The loan I'm making to the farm for improvements." He picked up another board and started to pound in a nail before glancing at Emma. Her eyes were huge and her mouth was wide open. Since she already appeared to be in shock, he decided to add the next item instead of waiting until later. Why have two arguments when he could have one? "Oh, you know that monthly salary Levi was paying you?"

"What about it?"

"Triple it." He continued to pound away long

after the nail was completely in. He was expecting fireworks from Emma; instead all he received was silence. Dead, eerie silence. When he couldn't stand it a moment longer, he asked, "Aren't you going to help?"

"Do you know what you're doing?" she countered as she watched him hammer in another nail.

"I haven't a clue." He handed her the hammer before the urge to pound in another nail overtook him again. "That's why we have a perfect partnership. You're the brains and I'm the brawn."

"You're also the one with the very deep pockets."

"Muscle and money are easy to obtain, Emma. It's your knowledge of chickens that has kept this farm from going under."

"Why is this farm so important to you all of a sudden?"

"What do you mean by 'all of a sudden'?"

"For the seven years I've been here, you never visited your grandfather, never called, and never even wrote. Now you're left with half of a bankrupted chicken farm and you start sinking money into it like there's no tomorrow."

"What do you know about my relationship with my grandfather?" It still hurt him after all these years that his grandfather had never responded to any of his letters.

"Not much. All I know is he kept your picture on his bureau until the day he died."

"What picture?"

"It looked like some school picture taken when you must have been around twelve. That's how come I knew you had your teeth straightened."

"Is the picture still around?" He couldn't believe it. His grandfather had cared somewhat for him if he had kept a picture all these years.

"After the funeral I packed up all of Levi's stuff and placed it in the spare bedroom, along with everything else he'd collected all his life." She pulled out the two nails Brent had just hammered in the boards. Neither one was doing any good. "When you get a chance, stop playing Martha Stewart and start going through all those boxes."

Very gingerly Emma set the rocker in motion. She wasn't sure if the ancient porch rocker had another summer in it, and she wasn't looking forward to kissing the wooden porch with her bottom. The sun was still over the mountains in the west, but it was sinking fast. The afternoon had sped by quickly with Brent helping her start to build the run and his constant questions about the farm, the town, and chickens. Always about chickens. What did they eat? Why that and not this? What vitamins, how much, and why? If she didn't know better, she would swear the man was actually going to become a chicken farmer.

The squeaking of the screen door alerted her to Brent's arrival. After spending a hot, sweltering afternoon working with her, he had insisted that she take a shower first while he cooked dinner. She in turn had allowed him the bathroom while she did the dishes and cleaned up the kitchen. By mutually unspoken word, they had both ended up on the porch again to watch the sunset.

"Would you like the rocker tonight?" Emma asked. It seemed only fair, considering she'd had it last night.

"That thing wouldn't hold my weight." Brent lowered himself to the top step, stretching his bare legs out and leaning back on one elbow. "I honestly don't see how it's even holding you." He turned his head to look at her, but his gaze didn't seem to lift higher than her legs.

"I don't weigh *that* much." She nervously shifted her legs and wished she had listened to herself earlier when deciding what to put on after her shower. The fearful woman inside her had pleaded for jeans and a baggy T-shirt, but common sense had won with its vote of shorts and a sleeveless blouse. It was still in the high eighties, and no amount of pleading could make her drag on heavy jeans again. Brent had to see her legs again sooner or later. Her brothers had teased her unmercifully about her legs while she was growing up. They had even nicknamed her "Giraffe" because of their length. For someone who was only five foot six, she felt as if her legs were six feet long.

"I was referring to the rocker's age and condition," Brent said, "not your weight." He turned his attention back to the picturesque view before them. "Do you realize how peaceful it is out here?"

"I have stepped off the farm a few times in my life, Haywood."

"Are you always so defensive?"

"I'm not being defensive, you're being condescending." At his look of surprise, she added, "Shocked you with that one, didn't I? I bet I could even spell it, and it has more than four letters."

He chuckled and shook his head. "I was surprised that you thought I was condescending, not that you know the word, Emma. If I had to be honest with myself, I would say I'm in awe of you."

"In awe of me?" she exclaimed. "Why?"

"You seem to know exactly what you want out of life and how to achieve it."

"I do?"

"Take this farm. You knew all along what it would take to make a go of it. Wasn't it you who convinced my grandfather to start raising chickens?"

"What does raising chickens have to do with what I want out of life?" She had taken the job Levi offered to get away from her drunken father and demanding brothers. Levi had given her the job because she knew a smidgen about farming and wasn't afraid of hard work, and because she was the only one who had applied. Raising chickens had absolutely nothing to do with her dreams. It was an honest, decent way to support herself and put food in her belly. Nothing more.

Brent's gaze never left her face. "What do you want out of life, Emma?"

She refused to meet his eyes. Instead she studied the fiery orange sun as it lowered slowly in the western sky. *What is it that I want out of life? she asked herself. A chance to dream. A home of my own. A family. Someone to love. Someone to love me. Nothing much, just the impossible.* All her life she had wanted those things and she had ended up with nothing, not even a second best. "It doesn't matter what you want out of life, Haywood. You take what you get and live with it."

"Are you just *living* with the chicken farm, Emma, because Levi left you half? Or is this something you want to do?"

"Is this a sneaky, citified way of finding out if I want to sell?" She gave him a quick glare before turning back to the setting sun.

"I wasn't offering to buy you out." He paused. "But if I were, would you sell?"

Would she sell? It was a hell of a question. Where would she go? Her couple of trips into Little Rock had convinced her she didn't like cities. There were just too many people, buildings, and noise. She did like the town of Strawberry Ridge, and she loved living out in the open, surrounded by green fields, clear skies, and blazing sunsets. She liked the good reputation the Amazing Grace Farm was obtaining for its high-quality chickens and the respect she was acquiring from the surrounding farming community. She still considered chickens one of the stupidest creatures the Lord had seen fit to put on this earth, but then again, she'd never seen a cow perform circus tricks. Would she sell Brent her half of the farm and everything she had been working toward for the last seven years?

She looked down at him. "Not in this lifetime, Haywood."

He chuckled. "I figured as much, but I wanted to make sure before I sank over twenty grand into the place."

"Do you really have that much cash lying around that you could make that size loan to the farm?"

"Lying around? No, but I can cash in a few stocks and bonds."

"What did you do before coming to Arkansas? Run numbers, handle a few contract killings, hit the lottery?" Her gaze caressed his body, and she almost added "be a gigolo" to the list. She had thought Brent was drop-dead gorgeous in faded jeans and damp, clingy T-shirts. But that was nothing to the cool, sophisticated look he projected while sitting on the old porch steps. His legs were tanned and muscular and were covered in brown curly hair that she longed to touch. His broad shoulders seemed to stretch the fabric of his pullover shirt to its limits, and the tightness of the shirt emphasized the flatness of his stomach.

"None of the above," he answered her. "You have a wicked imagination, Emma."

"It's from watching *Hill Street Blues* reruns."

She watched his fingers nervously crease the cuff on his khaki shorts, aware that it was his turn to refuse to meet her gaze. He seemed to be hiding something. A sense of unease shivered down her spine. Who exactly was her new partner? All she knew for sure was he was Levi's grandson. The geeky looking kid in the photo was definitely Brent. She could tell by the almost silver eyes and the irresistible dimple that creased his right cheek whenever he smiled. But what kind of man was Brent? For all she knew, he could be a wanted fugitive, an ax murderer, a bigamist with five different wives. "Hey, Haywood, what exactly did you do before coming down here to scope out your inheritance?"

His gaze never left the cuff of his shorts as he mumbled, "Modeling."

Emma stopped rocking and tried staring a hole in his back. She had to have misunderstood. He couldn't have said modeling. "What was that?"

He cleared his throat and looked over his shoulder at her. "I said, modeling."

A loud laugh escaped her throat as tears of mirth filled her eyes. "Did you say modeling?"

"What's wrong with modeling?" His voice hardened in defense. "It's an honest profession."

"I didn't say there was anything wrong with it, I just never knew anyone who had ever done it." She tried to control her laughter before she insulted him again and he reconsidered his loan, but a wayward giggle escaped anyway.

"I didn't know any chicken farmers before meeting you, and I don't remember bursting into laughter then."

Emma bit the inside of her cheek to stop any further unexpected snickers. She didn't know why his profession had surprised her, considering his looks, but it had. There seemed to be a lot more to Brent than just a beautiful face, a sexy grin, and an incredible body. "What did you do, model clothes for catalogs and such?"

He hesitated a moment before replying, "Something like that."

"Do you still do it?"

"No, I left it all behind when I left New York."

"So what do you do now?"

"It would seem I'm into raising chickens, Miss Emma."

FIVE

Emma opened the door of the spare bedroom and flipped on the light switch. The room was a nice size, and every square inch of it was crammed with boxes and old furniture. She squeezed her way into the room and pointed out three boxes stacked on top of each other near the door. "Those contain all of Levi's clothes that I cleared out of his bedroom." She removed a small cardboard box from the top of the pile and handed it to Brent. "Here are all the personal papers and photos he had in his room."

Brent took the box but didn't open it. He couldn't get over the idea of his grandfather displaying his sixth grade picture on his bureau for all those years. As soon as the sun had set, he had asked Emma to show him the photo. Of course, he'd had an ulterior motive. He didn't want his old profession brought up again. For some reason he had allowed Emma to presume he'd made his living posing for J.C. Penney's newest line, instead of admitting he had been one of the top male models in New York. It wasn't as if he was ashamed of what he did for a living. It just seemed so superficial, making indecent amounts of money all those years while his grandfather struggled daily to make ends meet.

"Why didn't you get rid of the clothes?" he asked, waving his hand at the other boxes. "On second thought, why didn't you just clean house totally? My grandmother's old sewing room, in back of the living room, would make a nice office."

"Levi refused to get rid of anything of your grandmother's. I believe he closed the door on the sewing room the day your grandmother passed on, and only opened it to store more things in it."

"My grandmother passed away over forty years ago." He shook his head at the room full of stuff. For almost half a century Levi had been hoarding memories of a wife he must have loved dearly. Brent wondered what it would be like to have loved someone so much that years later you couldn't bear to part with any of her possessions. "I can understand why Levi might not have wanted to toss any of this stuff, but why didn't you?"

"It seemed too personal to go sorting through all these boxes. I was only the hired hand. You're family."

"So I get the job?" For a moment he wasn't sure he wanted it. The task seemed monstrous and endless. Between this room, the sewing room, the basement, and the attic, he'd be lucky if his grand-children wouldn't be old enough to help him by the time he'd finished. But he couldn't think of a better way of getting to know his grandfather now that he was gone. And wasn't that one of the main reasons for coming there? Here was his opportunity to dis-cover a bit of his roots. Surely there had to be pic-tures, scrapbooks, mementos that would cast some light on this side of his heritage.

When he'd requested it the year before, his fa-ther's lawyer had sent him all the appropriate back-ground information. The Haywoods could trace their bloodline back to some long-forgotten earl in England. The lawyer seemed to have thought that would satisfy Brent. It hadn't. For months Brent had spent all of his free time, which wasn't much, in libraries gathering information about the Hay-woods. The more he learned, the more disgusted he became. The Haywoods came from lots of money, spent lots of money, and the current gener-ation did as little as possible to maintain its lofty position in society. The Haywoods stepped on or brushed aside anything that was inconsequential, and that had included him and his mother. Of course, his mother had gained financially, and the trust fund his father had set up for him was gener-ous enough. Brent never touched the fund, though, and the Haywood name still left a bad taste in his mouth. He was counting on his mother's side of the family to have some redeeming qualities.

His mother refused to talk about her "deprived

childhood," as she liked to refer to it. Her father was a taboo subject, and she only mentioned her mother occasionally. Brent knew that Grace Patterson had married Levi James at the tender age of seventeen. Years later they had a daughter, and Grace, who suffered from a weak heart, passed away one afternoon while helping Levi in the fields. Brent's mother blamed Levi and the farm for killing her mother and never forgave either. That didn't give Brent much understanding of his grandparents.

He glanced down at the box clutched in his hands and smiled. He was looking forward to unearthing his roots.

"Your letters are all in there," Emma said.

"My letters?"

"I found them in the nightstand when I cleaned out the room." She nodded toward the box he held. "By the postmarks I would guess you wrote them about the same time the picture was taken."

He frowned at the box. His grandfather had saved all his boyish attempts at communicating with a grouchy, stubborn man. Why, when he had never bothered to respond to any of them?

"Why did you stop writing?" Emma asked.

Brent's voice was heavy with all the pain he had felt years before. "He never once wrote me back."

"Did you expect him to?" Emma asked in surprise.

"It's logical that one would expect a letter in return once in a while."

Emma stood silent for a moment, studying him. "You didn't know, did you?"

Brent raised his head, straightened his shoulders, and shook off the pain of rejection. "Know what?"

"Levi couldn't read or write."

Brent felt as if the floor had moved under him. "What do you mean, he couldn't read or write?"

"Just what I said. He couldn't read or write."

"But the books downstairs?" he asked in confusion. How could he not have known his own grandfather was illiterate?

"I've been doing the books since the day I started. Over the years, Levi became very proficient at numbers. He managed to write checks, pay bills, and basically fool anyone who didn't know any better. I offered to teach him to read a couple of times, but Levi was a stubborn man. He kept saying that he hadn't needed to learn all those fancy words and letters up to this point in his life, so why start now."

Brent looked back down at the box. "So he never read any of my letters?"

"He never read them, but knowing Levi, I would say he had the preacher read them to him."

"What preacher?"

"The one who said a few words over his grave and laid him to rest. About once a month or so, the preacher used to stop by, trying to draw Levi back into the folds of the church. Levi used to pretend to think about it, until the preacher had read anything that Levi might have received since his last visit, and then Levi would show him the door. I think it was a game those two enjoyed playing. I witnessed it a couple of times, but the preacher stopped coming around as much once he realized Levi had me to read to him."

"Did the preacher ever write letters for my grandfather?"

"I'm afraid Levi was either too proud or stubborn to ask."

Brent now had his answer as to why his grandfather had never written him. Pride. His grandfather's pride had cost him a relationship with his grandson. Brent had been too young to suspect any other reason besides his grandfather's disliking him for not writing back. He sadly shook his head. "All those wasted years."

Emma awkwardly shrugged and shifted her bare feet on the wooden floor. "I'm going to go downstairs and see what's for dessert. Why don't you take your time and come down when you're ready." She quickly stepped from the room and went downstairs.

Brent glanced around the room in helpless confusion. If he hadn't known something that important about his grandfather, how was he ever going to piece together their lives? The task before him seemed insurmountable. He needed Emma's help. She had lived with Levi for seven years. She must have known the man better than his own daughter. With Emma's help, maybe he could fill in some of the blanks that made up his heritage. Once he knew where he had been, perhaps he could figure out where to go with his life. With a heavy sigh he shut off the lights and closed the door. Still carrying the box, he headed downstairs toward dessert, his future, and Emma.

Emma found the apple pie Brent had picked up in town that morning and set it out on the counter while she started a pot of coffee. Now that the sun had set and an evening breeze had developed, it was cooling down enough for the hot beverage. She shook her head in amazement as she slapped a filter into the old coffeemaker.

Brent was a model. Correction, he had been a model. She knew he was handsome enough to make a living off his looks, it had just never occurred to her that he had. *A model!* How could a man possibly go from posing in front of cameras to cleaning out chicken coops? It didn't seem natural. It didn't seem right. In fact, it seemed ludicrous. But she couldn't think of one good reason why Brent was staying and willing to sink a hefty chunk of cash into the farm unless he wanted to.

Maybe being a model wasn't as glamorous as she thought. Maybe Brent had had ambitions of becoming one of those really big models, the kind that flew from country to country, was invited to all sorts of fancy parties, and went around with an internationally known actress draped across each arm, and he'd never made it. She couldn't imagine someone with his looks being lost in the barrel with the rest of the male models, but from what she had seen on television, New York was brimming with gorgeous men, all competing for fame and glory. Maybe the rat race had become too much for him and he'd decided to chuck it all for the glamorous life of a gentleman chicken farmer.

Emma chuckled and reached for two cups as the coffee dripped its way through the filter. What did it matter to her what Brent used to do before coming to Strawberry Ridge? With him there doing half the work, she was beginning to feel as if she were on vacation. Instead of working sixteen hours a day, she was only putting in around ten. She even had had the time to catch up on all the odd jobs that had been overlooked for so long, and she still had a couple of hours each evening to relax. She should be dancing in the fields that Levi's grandson was willing to spend some money on the place. Any improvements he made benefited her too; after all, she was half owner of the farm.

She glanced into the darkened dining room and frowned. She was also half owner of the house, and so far Brent had been the one doing all the fixing up. Didn't she live there too? Not only should she have half the say in how the rooms should look, but she should be doing half the work. If not all the work, considering Brent was footing the bill.

She finishing setting the kitchen table and walked into the dining room, turning on the light as she went. Brent had thrown a lot of stuff out the night before. Scattered across the wooden table were his grandmother's fine china, two silver candlesticks, and an assortment of odds and ends. There were also the paint chips he had shown her that morning along with a few catalogs. Curious, she flipped open a catalog and immediately turned to the men's clothing section. Page after page of handsome men posed, smiled, and modeled the latest fashions, and not one of them was Brent. She frowned and opened the other catalog, passed the sheets and curtains, and stopped when she got to men's clothing. Brent wasn't in there either. She couldn't believe it. He was much more handsome than three-quarters of those models, and the other quarter he could beat hands down when he flashed that sexy, I'm-going-to-love-you-like-you've-never-been-loved-before grin of his.

"What are you looking for?" Brent asked as he walked into the room. He placed the small box she'd given him upstairs on the table.

Emma jumped at the sound of his voice and immediately slammed the catalog closed. "Chri—" She noticed his amused expression and quickly changed the word she was about to say. "Christmas, Brent, what did I tell you about sneaking up on a person?"

"I was hoping for a third I.O.U."

"There aren't going to be any I.O.U.'s, Haywood." Here she was actually feeling sorry for the guy and he goes and blows it with ridiculous talk about I.O.U.'s for kisses.

He glanced at the catalog. "Did you pick out curtains?"

She pushed the catalogs away and stomped her foot. "Don't you dare change the subject, Haywood."

"What subject would that be?"

"The asinine notion that you can collect a kiss every time I feel like swearing." She jammed her hands onto her hips and glared at him. Most women would probably consider her to be the asinine one for not cursing up a storm. In fact, with Brent's looks she should be inventing new ones to burn his ears with instead of fighting him. The problem was, she liked his kisses a little too well.

"I once knew a guy who every time he cursed, he had to put a quarter in a jar." Brent walked into the kitchen and found an old mayonnaise jar in one of the cabinets. He set it on top of the refrigerator and started to rummage through the catch-all drawer.

"I'll be broke before the end of the week," Emma said, "if I have to drop a quarter in that jar every time you provoke me into cussing."

Brent found paper, a pair of scissors, and a red felt-tipped marker. He started to cut the paper into two-inch squares. "I know." He drew a big X on each square, dropped two into the jar, and placed the rest neatly in the drawer. "I only made up two dozen I.O.U.'s so far."

A flush swept up her cheeks. "This is my house, too, and if I feel like swearing, I will!"

"It's half mine." His gaze lingered on her lips. "I can think of a dozen things you could do with your mouth, and cursing isn't one of them."

The flush turned brilliant red, not out of embarrassment, but from excitement. The heated look in his eyes was telling her exactly what he wanted to do with her mouth, and her treacherous body was melting like cotton candy upon her tongue. Brent Haywood had to be the devil in disguise. Who else could make her want something she knew was bad for her? She shook her head and forced herself not to look at his mouth. The best defense was a quick offense. "Well, you have annoying habits too." Her finger lightly tapped him on the chest. "And you don't see me passing out I.O.U.'s."

"What habits?" He looked at her finger as it tapped him again.

"Oodles of them," she lied. At this particular moment she couldn't think of one blasted thing the man did wrong or that annoyed her. She was damn lucky she was thinking at all, considering he was less than a foot away and her bones had the consistency of overcooked noodles.

A smile played at one corner of his mouth. "Name them."

"You add too much salt to everything you cook." She tapped his chest yet again to emphasize her point. "You drink imported beer when every redneck chicken farmer in America knows to drink beer brewed in the good old U.S. of A." Her voice rose and her finger continued to tap as he flashed her his killer grin. Totally flustered, she forgot what she was about to say and ended up shouting, "And that sexy smile of yours has to go!" Her finger stopped in mid-tap when she realized what she'd said.

Brent's grin grew larger as he captured her wayward finger. "Ah, Emma, you do care."

She yanked her finger out of his hand and glared back at him. "Get *¢&%$!"

He opened the drawer, pulled out a square with a red X marked on it, and dropped it into the jar. "There's three."

"You can drop all the slips of papers you want into the jar, but it doesn't mean I'm honoring them." The man was impossible!

"I'd never force you, Emma. You should know that by now." His smile became gentle and understanding. "I'll wait until you're ready to pay up."

"Hell will freeze over before I'd honor some stupid I.O.U."

He sadly shook his head and dropped another piece of paper into the jar. "Four."

Emma's chin rose a notch as she threatened a vital part of his anatomy with unspeakable harm.

He calmly dropped more squares into the jar. "Five, six, and seven." He held the rest of the twenty-four squares in his hand and raised an eyebrow. "Shall we try for an even dozen?" He shook his head at her reply and dropped two more into the jar. "Eight and nine."

The words that erupted from her mouth caused him to chuckle and continue to drop I.O.U.'s into the jar. "I must admit, Emma, I've never heard them strung together so creatively."

By the time she controlled her unruly tongue and her temper, Brent was holding one last slip of paper. Furious with herself, him, and her luck, she snapped her mouth closed. It was just her luck to have been sent the devil himself disguised as a godsend. There was no way she was honoring those I.O.U.'s. There was no way he could make her. Without saying a word, she turned around and started to march out of the kitchen.

"If this continues, partner," he called after her, "I'm afraid we're going to run out of paper real soon."

She hesitated on the stairs as his words reached her. Her bare toes connected with the next step as she growled what he could do with his paper and his little red Xs.

"I heard that, Emma," came floating up from the kitchen. "That makes it an even two dozen."

The slamming of her bedroom door vibrated the entire house.

Brent glanced at the kitchen clock. It was after midnight. For the past two hours he had been sitting alone in the kitchen drinking the coffee Emma had made and going through the box of papers his grandfather had kept in his bedroom. Personal papers. Papers that gave him another glimpse of the man he'd never really known. Papers that showed him exactly how much his grandfather had cared about him. Every one of his letters had been saved and cherished. He could tell they had been handled quite a lot through the years.

The sixth grade picture was one he had sent his grandfather. It wasn't a very good photo. His mother had taken one look at it and his other school photos, thrown them away, and taken him to a private studio to have them redone. He had snuck the one photo from the trash can and mailed it to his grandfather. Levi had kept it all these years.

Tears filled Brent's eyes as he studied his grandparents' wedding photo, taken over half a century ago. The black-and-white photo showed a young couple, obviously deeply in love, standing on the steps of a church. This was his heritage.

The box also contained an assortment of photos of his mother, from her first baby picture to her high school graduation photo. She had been an ordinary looking baby, and adolescence looked to have been as awkward for her as it had been for him. By the time she was about fifteen, though, there was a marked difference in her appearance. The little duckling had turned into a swan. Her graduation photo was perfection. She had a face that could capture the world, or at least a very rich husband. And it had. By the time she was twenty she had married a blue-blooded Haywood. Over the years, she had only moved upward with each husband.

Brent held a faded photo of his grandmother and his mother's high school graduation picture side by side. Except for the hairstyle, they could have been the same girl, or at least sisters. His grandmother had been a very beautiful woman.

He slowly repacked everything into the box. What did it matter what they looked like? He knew how unimportant looks were. They didn't make a person, but they seemed to be what everyone first judged a person on.

The most courageous, hardworking, and fascinating woman he had ever met wasn't breathtakingly beautiful. His gaze raised to the ceiling and he smiled. But she was attractive and a bit on the wild side. Emma stirred desires he hadn't known existed until he arrived in Arkansas. What in the world was he going to do about her? She was more skittish than a newborn colt. One minute she was looking at him as if he were dessert, and the next, nothing but confusion clouded her big blue eyes. It was driving him crazy.

He still could picture the fear he'd glimpsed on her face when he had kissed her. He dismissed the notion that Emma had never been kissed before straight out of his head. She was too vibrant and alive not to have attracted men. So what had caused the fear? Him? The intense desire that had exploded between them? Something from her past? All he knew was she had been afraid of something.

There was no way he was going to ignore the attraction sizzling between them, but he wasn't going to push it either. At least, not until he found out what had caused her fear. He wanted her to feel safe in her own home. The best solution he could come up with was to make light of the kiss, while keeping it fresh in her mind. The I.O.U.'s for swearing were a stroke of brilliance on his part, if he did say so himself. He might have pushed it a little too far that night, but it was either keep teasing her, or haul her into his arms and kiss her speechless. It had twisted his gut when she'd responded to his kiss with fear. If it happened again, he was afraid it would tear his heart.

Over the last week Emma Carson had become more than just a partner, she had become a thief. She had stolen a piece of his heart, and he was very much afraid he would never get it back.

Emma moved farther into the shadows and watched Brent. He had climbed the small hill overlooking the farm and sat beneath an old maple tree, and he seemed to be staring down at the farm. She couldn't see his eyes, but he had to be watching something.

For the past week he had been sorting through all the stuff that had been stashed in his grandmother's sewing room and the spare bedroom upstairs. So far he had made two trips to the dump and one trip to the local church to donate boxes of clothes to the needy. She had never seen a man more obsessed with finding his roots. Every scrap of paper had to be read, and there were boxes filled with all kinds of papers. He questioned her endlessly about Levi, and most of the questions she couldn't answer. Levi had been a private person who never talked about himself or the past. In the seven years she had known him, he'd only mentioned Brent's mother once, and his wife twice. Until near the end. After he became bedridden and he knew the end was approaching, he'd talked about his Gracie, as he liked to call her, frequently. He'd once told her that Gracie had the face of an angel, the heart of a saint, and could outbake every woman in the county. The Amazing Grace Farm bore her name because she had been the one who talked Levi into investing every penny they had into the land and their future. It had ripped Emma's heart up to see tears in the old coot's eyes whenever he mentioned her.

The previous night Brent had discovered his grandmother's diary buried in the bottom of a box. Emma had gone to bed while he had been sitting at the kitchen table reading it. That morning he had been awfully quiet during breakfast, and he had been acting strangely all day. Whatever he had read in the diary must have upset him. Emma had a feeling she knew what it was.

She stepped out of the shadows, slowly climbed

the hill to the big maple tree, and sat down beside him. The sweet smell of newly cut hay from the field below filled the air. Emma stretched out her legs and removed her baseball cap, allowing her golden braid to swing free. That morning, after a few days of reprieve, the heat had returned.

She glanced at Brent and suppressed a smile. He was beginning to look like a farmer. His new boots were scuffed and caked with dirt, and his jeans looked worn from hard work, not some factory acid washing. His brown hair was in need of a trim, and he was wearing a white baseball cap with the emblem of a motor oil across its front. His light blue T-shirt was tight enough to outline every fascinating detail of his chest and shoulders. She knew every inch of his upper body. She had devoured it with her gaze enough times that she could close her eyes and picture it in delectable detail. The first time she had run across him working outside without a shirt, she'd nearly had heart failure. The thought of him having an accident and marring such perfection had her begging him to put his shirt back on. When he'd refused, she had earned herself two more I.O.U.'s and his sexy grin.

The I.O.U.'s didn't bother her, because she knew Brent would never force the issue. In a way she was confused as to why he never demanded payment after collecting them so vigorously. Or why he bothered at all. And why kisses and not quarters? Why accumulate a jar full of kisses and not collect them? Quarters he could use, but kisses?

A kiss was something a person wanted, and he obviously didn't want hers. Or did he? A couple of times she had caught a strange gleam in his silver eyes. A gleam that had nothing to do with their being partners, and everything to do with him being a man and her being a woman. Emma shook her head and looked up at the hand-size leaves above her. She'd never realized how overactive her imagination could be until she imagined Brent wanting to kiss her. Lord, the next thing she knew she'd be chasing pixies across the hay fields and dancing naked under the full moon.

"What's so funny?" Brent asked.

She hadn't realized she'd chuckled out loud until he spoke. "Nothing, just laughing at myself." She picked a blade of grass and stuck it in her mouth as Brent went back to staring down at the farm. The improvements made since he had arrived were everywhere. The lawn surrounding the house was neatly mowed, bushes and trees had been trimmed, and he had even planted a few flowers near the porch. At one time Grace had had huge flower gardens all around the house, but now most of them had gone back to grass.

Brent had shown her a photo of the house taken a year or so after it had been built. He wanted to restore it to its former glory. Secretly she thought a bulldozer might do a better job with the sagging porch than a hammer and nails. Still, she had to admit the whole place was looking better. After endless trips to the dump, most of the junk that had littered the yard and the barn had been hauled away. Freshly washed sheets were hung on the clothesline, and Brent had paid someone from town to spread tons of gravel along the driveway, from the highway to the house. The new run behind the barn had been built at the expense of two more rolls of chicken wire and a couple of sheets of plywood. Nearly sixty chickens occupied the new enclosure. The future of the Amazing Grace Farm looked bright. Now if only her partner would smile.

She glanced over at him. "Want to talk about it?"

He plopped his chin on his knees, still staring down at the house. After what seemed like minutes, he said, "She had known all along."

Emma felt her heart lurch at the sadness in his voice. She knew what he was referring to. After spending all those hours discovering his grandparents, he now was feeling the impact of their deaths. Grace James had known for years that her heart was giving out and had never once told Levi. "She didn't want Levi fussing and worrying over every little thing she did."

Brent quickly raised his head and stared at her. "You knew?"

"Levi told me." She pulled her knees up and matched his position. "During the last couple weeks of his life, Levi used to sit for hours and talk to me." She glanced down at the house. "I don't know if it was the medication he was on, or if he was just plain old scared, but he talked for hours into the night." She could feel the tears start to build and swallowed hard. "Most nights he talked until dawn."

"Why didn't he stop her from doing so much?"

"He didn't know until she died. She had made the doctor promise not to tell Levi, because there wasn't anything he or the medical profession could do. She had wanted to live whatever time God allowed her as a normal wife and mother."

"That's what her diary said." Brent shrugged helplessly. "But still . . ."

"Still what?" Emma raised an eyebrow and glared at him. "Are you going to blame Levi, just like your mother did? The man *did not* know, and for the rest of his life he had to live with the knowledge that the woman he loved had never told him. She died in his arms, in the middle of a field she had no right being in, doing work she had no business doing." She swiped at the tears rolling down her face. "Try living with that one!"

She could still remember the night Levi had told her about Gracie's death and how he'd cried. Levi, the grouchy old goat who didn't care a hoot about anything or anyone, had cried like a baby in her arms. She'd had no words to comfort him, only an awkward embrace. Levi had seemed to be more peaceful after that. Two days later he'd joined his Gracie.

"I wasn't blaming my grandfather, Emma. After reading my grandmother's diary, I feel as if I had known her. I can understand her pain and why she didn't tell her husband. She loved him more than life itself." He reached out and tenderly captured a tear that was creeping down her cheek. "You liked old Levi, didn't you?"

"I guess you could say he was the grandfather I never had."

"No grandfathers?"

"No grandfathers, no grandmothers, and since I was three, no mother." She turned her head away from his hand. "I was raised by an alcoholic father and three older brothers whose main objectives in life are hunting, fishing, wild women, and cold beer." He might as well hear it from her instead of some old biddy in town who had nothing better to do than gossip about Emma Carson's upbringing. If Brent ever visited any of the local watering holes, he was sure to run across one of her brothers. Ever since the day she'd moved out and they'd had to start fending for themselves, none of them had had a nice word to say about their little sister. Then again, none of them had had a nice word to say about her when she did live there.

"My God, Emma."

She smiled at the horror in his voice. The expression on his face was priceless. One would think she had been raised by Jack the Ripper and Charles Manson. "Why, Brent, I do believe you owe me an I.O.U." she teased.

His initial look of surprise turned thoughtful as he studied the playful smile tugging at her mouth.

"Any time you're willing to collect, I'm willing to pay up."

Emma noticed the sudden stillness about him. Not a muscle moved. He didn't even seem to be breathing as he waited for her response. Should she kiss him? Dare she kiss him and see what happened? She did trust Brent not to hurt her, and ever since the first kiss, she had been dreaming about more of them. There was no way it could be as great as she remembered. Her gaze caressed his mouth and the sharp edge of his jaw. Oh, how she wanted to taste his mouth, just one more time. "It should only be a little kiss, since it was only a little curse."

Brent's fist clenched around a handful of grass. "You set the pace." His gaze never left her face as she bent forward and brushed her mouth against his. He raised one eyebrow. "You call that a kiss?"

Emma pulled back and frowned. That hadn't gone as she had planned. She leaned forward and pressed a harder kiss upon his mouth. Getting no response from Brent struck something deep down inside her. She wanted a kiss from him, a real, honest-to-goodness kiss. She wanted his response.

With a sigh she traced his lower lip with the tip of her tongue and threaded her fingers into his hair, knocking off his baseball cap. She pulled back a fraction of an inch and whispered, "Kiss me back, Brent."

The fistful of grass was yanked from the earth as he parted her mouth and answered her plea.

SIX

Brent had thought he would never again experience the heated desire that had erupted in his body the first time he had kissed Emma. He'd been wrong. It was happening again. And this time Emma was the one who'd initiated the explosion. Her sweet, tentative kiss was searing its way into his heart. The clump of grass fell from his hand as he drew her closer and gave her the response she asked for.

She sighed as his mouth took command of the kiss. Her fingers trembled in his hair, and her breasts pressed against his solid chest as she moved closer still. When his tongue parted her lips, she allowed him entrance and opened the gates to paradise.

Wave after wave of heat rolled through his body, cresting and crashing, sucking him into the undertow of desire. Her name was torn from his lips in a half curse, half prayer. He wanted her like no other woman, but he remembered her fear and tried to pull back.

She moaned in protest and crushed her body against his until he fell onto his back. Their weight was cushioned by a sweet-smelling patch of clover and grass. Somewhere overhead a bird started to sing, but Brent didn't hear its song. He only heard the pounding of his heart and Emma's kittenlike purrs, and he deepened the kiss. Her body lying across his felt like heaven. It felt right. He absorbed the shudder that shook her, then released her mouth and opened his eyes.

He watched anxiously as Emma opened her own eyes and stared down at him. Her flushed face was warm with desire, her lips were swollen and moist, and her eyes held nothing but wonder and a silent question, asking him why he had stopped. There wasn't a trace of fear anywhere. He reached up and brushed a few wisps of golden hair, that had escaped her braid, back behind her ear. "Do you want me to stop?"

Desire rocketed through his body as she smiled and shook her head. He cupped her face and caressed her sun-kissed cheek with his thumb. "How do you keep your skin so soft?"

"Soap and water." She moved her head so that his thumb touched her lips.

"I figured that, since I share the same bathroom with you." His thumb parted her lips and outlined the moist underside of the lower one. "I know women who spend a fortune on moisturizers and creams praying to achieve this effect. They never do."

Her smile faded, but she didn't pull back. "They should save their money and be content with what God gave them."

Brent gave a harsh laugh. "Models are never *content* with their looks, Emma. It's their career not to be."

"What about you?"

"What about me?" His fingers trailed down the side of her neck and tilted her face upward, allowing him access to her throat. His lips nuzzled the soft skin, and he once again marveled at its smoothness.

"You don't seem too preoccupied with your looks." She clung to his shoulders as his mouth slid down closer to her breasts.

He chuckled and skimmed a string of kisses along the neck of her T-shirt. "Thanks." His lips traced the contour of her collarbone. "I think."

His fingers trailed over her shoulders and down her tanned arms. Golden hairs, bleached lighter by the sun, tickled the tips of his fingers. His gaze followed his fingers until they reached her hands. Strong, capable hands that lay trembling against his chest. His gaze rose to the woman above him. To the gentle arch of her throat. To the silkiness of her golden braid draped over her shoulder. To the hunger burning in her blue eyes. And to the lush curves of her breasts straining against the brilliant white of her shirt.

Sometime after lunch Emma had changed out of the dusty red shirt she had worn that morning to cut hay. She had also washed up and rebraided her hair. He had been noticing subtle changes in her over the past few days. The rough edges were changing into feminine curves. The curves had always been there, he was sure. Only now they were more noticeable and had the disquieting ability to cost him hours of sleep.

He placed his hands on her waist and slowly slid them upward. He could feel the warmth of her skin beneath the shirt, the contour of her body, and the quick breaths she was taking. His gaze remained on her face. He wanted to gauge her reaction to his touch. He needed to know if the fear would return.

She sucked in a sharp breath and arched her back more as his palms caressed the sides of her breasts. All he would have to do was lift his head a few inches off the soft bed of clover and he could capture one of the hardening peaks pushing against the soft cotton. Those taut nipples gave him hope. Emma wasn't immune to his touch. She wanted this as much as he did.

Days of frustration had taken their toll. With one lithe movement he arched his body off the ground and reversed their positions. Emma was lying in the clover and he was propped up on his side staring down at her flushed face. His hand toyed with the hem of her T-shirt, which had been pulled from the waistband of her jeans by his sudden movement. He swept a kiss across her lips as the tip of his finger stroked the narrow strip of skin left exposed above the waistband. Heat branded his fingertip.

His mouth made another sweeping pass across hers as his palm flattened against her stomach. He could feel her muscles clench and willed his body to slow down. When she made a soft sound of distress, he immediately opened his eyes and moved back. His heart gave a painful lurch when he saw the fear had returned to her eyes. "Emma?"

She scooted a foot away from him, yanked down her T-shirt, and wildly stared at the tree above, the hazy sky, the house below, anywhere but at him. She took a couple of ragged breaths and blurted out a shaky, "I'm sorry."

"For what?" He pushed his fingers through his hair and forced his voice to remain calm. Emma was afraid of him! He had never harmed a person in his life, and to have her fear directed at him was confusing. He didn't know what to do or say. The first thing he had to do was figure out what she was afraid of, then maybe he could make some sense out of this whole thing.

"This"—she waved an arm at where they had just been lying—"should never have happened."

"Why?"

"Why?"

He tilted his head and studied her body. There was no denying her response to his kisses. She wanted them as much as he wanted to give them. Her nipples weren't hard because of a chill. It was ninety-six in the shade, and the heat they had just generated was enough to melt steel. "Yes, Emma, why?" He frowned as she nervously tugged at the grass. "Are you afraid this is going to complicate our partnership?" It seemed a reasonable assumption, but not drastic enough to cause the fear he had witnessed.

"Our partnership?" she repeated in confusion. She stared down at the house, the barn, and the assorted chicken runs dotting the land. After a moment she shook her head as if the idea had never occurred to her before. "No, Brent, this had nothing to do with our business dealings. But you're right. Partners shouldn't go around necking under a tree."

"I didn't say partners shouldn't kiss." He wasn't about to let her turn this around on him. "I want to know what happened that made you afraid."

"Who said anything about me being afraid?" Her chin rose a notch and she finally looked at him.

Brent knew he should have disintegrated on the spot if her look had anything to do with it. He had hit a nerve. "No one said anything about you being afraid, Emma. But I do have eyes, and something caused that fear I saw in you."

"Do you know what I think?" She stood up and brushed off the seat of her jeans. "I think you need glasses." With a flip of her hand she sent her thick braid flying behind her shoulder. "Just because I thought things were getting a little out of hand, you have to jump to the conclusion I was afraid."

"Weren't you?"

"The kiss was fine."

"Fine!" Brent choked and sputtered. If the kiss had gotten any hotter, it would have singed the clover.

"Okay, maybe 'fine' is too polite. The kiss was great, super, fantastic. If I had to grade it on a scale of one to ten, it was a nine, okay?"

Hurt by the low rating, he asked, "Just a nine?" If he had been keeping score, he would have given it a twelve.

"Listen, Brent, it was a great kiss. Let's leave it at that. Now it's time to get back to work. This farm doesn't run itself. Someone has to move about six hens and fifty chicks out of the nesting building and into the nursery."

"You're not going to tell me, are you?" She was denying the fear too vigorously. She had been afraid, and she knew it. The Emma he had grown to know didn't seem to be afraid of anything. He had seen her chase a hungry fox off in the middle of the night with a shotgun. He had seen her work from sunup to sundown without a complaint. He had seen her trap and kill a rat that had been after the chicken feed in the barn. He had also seen her cuddle and play with the chicks when she thought no one was looking.

"There is nothing to tell, Haywood." She turned around and started down the hill.

"You're going to have to tell me sooner or later,

Emma. I'm not going away, and I'm not giving up."

Her feet faltered and she came to a stop. Without turning around, she said, "I'm not a tease, Haywood."

"I never said you were."

She gave a slight nod and continued down the hill to the nesting building.

Brent watched until she disappeared inside the building, then plopped himself back down on the grass. Frustration and passion still raced through his body, with no outlet in sight. He threw his arm over his eyes and shut out the sunlight. His head was beginning to pound. What in the hell did Emma mean, she wasn't a tease? He'd never said she was, never even thought it. Was that what she was afraid of? That he would think she was a tease for calling a halt?

No, that couldn't be it. And Emma wasn't afraid of him, he was sure of that. If she was, she would have pulled her knife and threatened to slice off something important. So that meant she had to be afraid of kissing or the desire that erupted between them. How in the hell was he going to combat that? Stop kissing her? Not in this lifetime.

There had to be another way to learn what had caused her fear. But what? Brent stood up and brushed some blades of grass from his clothes. His frustration level had dropped below the danger zone, but it was still in the active stage. Emma had that effect on him no matter what time of day or night it was.

He silently vowed to find the root of her fear and combat it for her if necessary. Emma shouldn't live with any fear. He started down the hill, watching her carrying a basket with a hen and her chicks from the nesting building to the nursery, where they would have plenty of room to roam. One question still plagued his mind. What did she mean, she wasn't a tease? It seemed awfully important to her that he knew she wasn't. Had someone in her past called her a tease when she said stop? Had that someone become a little too forceful and caused the fear he now witnessed?

Brent muttered an oath that would have surely earned him a couple of I.O.U.'s had Emma been listening. What he didn't need was for his imagination to start to conjure up stories. What he needed was for Emma to trust him enough to talk to him. He walked into the nesting building, picked up a basket, and went in search of a hen and her chicks.

Emma pushed her spaghetti around her plate and felt the knot of anxiety twisting tighter in her gut. She had lied to Brent. On the scale of one to ten, their kiss had been a twelve, and she had never felt more rotten in her life. To make it up to him, she had volunteered to cook dinner. It was pretty hard to mess up meat sauce, a bunch of noodles, and a salad. From the way Brent was eating it, one would think the man hadn't eaten in days.

He glanced up from his meal and grinned. "I thought you said you couldn't cook. This is great."

"I never said I couldn't. It's just that cooking isn't one of my favorite things to do." She pushed a noodle to the other end of her plate. Visions of her father flinging a plate of spaghetti against the wall just because the sauce was too runny, or there wasn't enough meat in it, or the noodles weren't cooked properly, still plagued her. The thought of Brent standing up, shouting, and flinging plates of spaghetti was about as realistic as little green men arriving from outer space to join them for dessert.

Brent was on the opposite side of the spectrum from her father, brothers, and the handful of men she knew. Until Brent had arrived, she had been convinced that Levi was as nice as a man ever got. His being a silent brooder and demanding taskmaster was easy enough to live with after her family. The men from town who treated her decently whenever she was in Strawberry Ridge gave her the creeps. They had to be hiding something, she was sure, just as Jack Roddman, the captain of her high school's football team, had been hiding a darker side.

All through high school the handsome and athletic Jack had captured her attention and starred in her schoolgirl fantasies. No boy had been stronger, braver, or more popular than Jack. Every girl from fourteen to twenty had a crush on him, and he had known it. He'd had his pick of girlfriends, and on the night of their high school graduation, he had picked her. Now, when she could look back on that night with more perspective, she knew where she'd gone wrong. She had allowed her treacherous young heart to hope that she was the girl who would win Jack's love and live out a dream.

The night had started at a keg party overflowing with loud music and an endless stream of beer. Jack had been an attentive date, making sure her cup was never empty. By midnight she had felt right at home at the party, and excited by the weight of Jack's body constantly pressing up against hers. When he suggested they split from the party and take a ride, she agreed. They ended up on a deserted road about five miles from town. At first his kisses thrilled her and she relished every one. Her experience with boys had been limited to the few who were brave enough to steal a kiss. Jack Roddman had been voted the best kisser by her senior class and she wanted to savor the experience.

When his hands started to wander, she began to get uncomfortable, but kept quiet. This was Jack Roddman after all. Her hazy, beer-clouded mind cleared when his hands became demanding. She told him no. He slapped her across the face, shouted that she was a tease, and took what he wanted. It had been five o'clock in the morning before she reached home with a swollen lip, a torn blouse, and shattered dreams. She'd lost a shoe, and her foot was cut and bruised from a six-mile hike along dark country roads. No one had cared enough to notice she hadn't spent the night in her bed. Within a week she began working for Levi.

Brent glanced at her full plate and frowned. "Aren't you hungry?"

She stared down at the spaghetti and felt sick to her stomach. Brent deserved the truth, and she didn't have the guts to tell him. How could she explain that it wasn't his kisses that she feared, it was the part that came afterward? The part where he changed from the Brent she liked and respected to another Jack Roddman. The first time Brent had kissed her, in the living room, she had felt his hard arousal and had known nothing but fear. That afternoon the fear had reappeared when he'd loomed over her. He was as tall and broad shouldered as Jack. She had realized that whatever Brent wanted, he could take just as easily as Jack had. She honestly didn't believe he would turn into another Jack, but the fear had been there regardless. It would be better for both of them if they kept their relationship strictly business and left the necking under trees to teenagers. She pushed aside her plate. "I had a pretty big lunch."

"Are you sure you're feeling okay?"

The one thing she didn't want was his concern. She didn't deserve it. "I'm fine, just a little tired." *Another lie.* What had she to be tired about? Since Brent had showed up, her workload had been cut in half and her salary tripled.

"Maybe you could use a couple days off."

"I'm not *that* tired." She pushed back her chair and stood. "I think I'll call it an early night, that's all." She had gotten less sleep before Brent arrived and had worked twice as hard. But at least then she hadn't dreamed.

"Tomorrow I need you to ride into Newport with me," he said.

"What for?" Newport was the nearest big town, and she could count on one hand the number of times she had walked its streets.

"We need to buy a new pickup truck and I want your opinion as to what it should have in it."

"You're going to buy a new truck?" She tried to keep the awe out of her voice.

"I'm still driving a rental from the airport, and the farm could definitely use a new truck. That hunk of rust you call a truck isn't going to last another trip to the dump."

"If you spend all the money on a truck, we won't have enough for the improvements." She would love a new truck. Hell, she would love a used truck with under one hundred and fifty thousand miles on it, but the expansions had to come first.

"The truck is for me, and I promise not to use a penny of the loan money for it."

"Oh." Now she understood. The truck was his. "So what do you need me for?"

"Because you probably have a hell of a lot more experience driving a pickup than me." He thrust his fingers through his hair in exasperation. "Listen,

Emma. I've never bought a pickup truck. Heck, I'd never even driven one till I came here." He gave her his famous grin. "And I'm still not sure if that rusted bundle of bolts constitutes a truck."

"It's a truck." She matched his grin. "Trust me." Anyone who had driven old Betsy and still had a sense of humor about it couldn't be all bad.

"I do trust you. That's why I'm asking for your help."

How could she possibly refuse him anything when he flashed that grin? Every bone in her body had about as much stand-up power as her dinner congealing on her plate. She would have driven to the gates of Hades to look at trucks with him. "We'll go after the chores are done." She scraped the food off her plate into the garbage pail and placed it in the sink. "But it's going to cost you."

"Anything."

She raised an eyebrow at the ideas his generosity gave her. She kept those thoughts to herself and answered, "Lunch."

Emma dug into her second order of french fries and smiled at Brent sitting across from her in the booth. "But this is exactly where I wanted to go," she said in answer to his question. She nodded toward a six-foot cardboard cutout of a fuzzy-haired clown wearing big red shoes. "The nearest you'll ever see old Ronald to Strawberry Ridge is thirty-four miles. Believe me, I clocked it one night when I had a french fry attack." She popped another fry into her mouth and chewed. "Old Betsy can't make the distance any longer, so I have to make do with the diner in town. Their fries just aren't the same."

"I would have splurged for something a bit more formal." Brent picked an empty straw wrapper off his shoulder and glared at the kid in the next booth who had just shot it at him.

Emma grinned at the kid. Brent needed to be knocked down a peg or two after the way Leon, the salesman from Bob's Truck Bonanza, had fawned all over him. She had been surprised Leon hadn't drooled. "You promised me my choice of restaurants."

"A deal is a deal." He took another bite from his burger. "Do you want to explain to me again what was wrong with that Ford pickup I was looking at?"

"Absolutely nothing was wrong with it, if the price included your own private chauffeur."

"I thought it was reasonably priced for what it had."

"Most of what it had, you don't need."

"Like what?"

She took a swallow of soda and washed down the last of the french fries. "Air-conditioning, for one."

"I need air-conditioning, Emma. Lord, it's almost a hundred degrees out there today, and it's only the beginning of May. By the time July gets here, Hades itself will be cooler."

"It's just a little heat wave, Brent." She glanced at the menu hanging above the cashiers and wondered if Brent would splurge for another round of fries. "Besides, if you want air, open the windows. The cost for them was at least included in the basic sticker price." She scowled at the young cashier who was making cow eyes at Brent.

"So you pointed out to the salesman."

"Speaking of our pal Leon, he was too pushy."

"It's his job to be pushy."

"No, it's his job to sell gullible city boys pretty red pickup trucks with CDs in them." She shook her head and finished off her drink.

"What's wrong with a CD player?"

"Nothing's wrong with a CD player, Brent, if you have CDs." She glanced at his french fries. "I personally think it's all a conspiracy to get people to buy things they don't really need. First they sold everyone eight-tracks, so everyone had to buy eight-track tapes. Then it was cassettes, now it's CDs." She swiped a fry. "In two years it will be something else."

"Emma?" He pushed his fries across the table toward her. "I already have CDs."

"You do?" She hadn't noticed any CDs or tapes lying around the house.

"They'll be arriving with the rest of my stuff by the end of the week."

"What kind of stuff?"

"Everything from my apartment."

"What do you mean by everything?"

"The rest of my clothes, a living room set, all my kitchen stuff, my stereo with the CDs and cassettes, a twenty-five-inch color TV, a VCR, my videotape collection, and my king-size water bed."

"You're kidding, right?"

"Afraid not."

With him living out of the two suitcases he had brought with him, she had never seriously considered him staying for the long haul. She had convinced herself he would be returning to the hustle and bustle of New York and the glamorous life of being a model. If he was going to all this trouble and expense to have everything shipped down here, he wasn't planning on going back. He had been dead serious about the loan and expanding the farm. Brent Haywood was staying in Arkansas, and the wall surrounding her heart would never stand the strain.

"Emma?"

"Huh?" Her gaze never left the third button on his shirt. Brent would be sleeping across the hall from her for the rest of her life. He would be showering in the same tub, using the same mirror. His toothbrush was side-by-side to hers. His underwear would be swishing around with hers in the same washer. There was no hope for it. She would be insane before the autumn harvest.

"Do you want another order of fries before we

go back over to Bob's Truck Bonanza and buy my truck?"

She looked down at the three empty packs on her tray and felt the heavy brick of deep-fried potatoes lying in the pit of her stomach. "No thanks. I think I had my limit."

SEVEN

Emma sat in the rickety old rocker and watched as three burly men and Brent unloaded the moving van. How one man could possess so much stuff was beyond her. They had been steadily hauling out furniture and boxes for the past forty-five minutes, and there didn't seem to be an end in sight. Brent must have inherited his grandfather's habit of never throwing anything out.

The big yellow moving van was backed up as close to the porch steps as possible, and Brent's shiny red pickup was parked right next to it. Old Betsy was parked proudly on the other side. Emma had to hand it to the old truck, because Brent had been wrong. Not only had she made another trip to the dump without conking out, she had made another six.

In the four days since Brent had purchased his new truck, he had become obsessed with getting the house ready for his furniture. The old master bedroom furniture was now set up in the spare bedroom, leaving the larger room empty. Brent had told Emma the living room was hers to do with whatever she wanted. She had saved two small tables and an old floor lamp and put them in her bedroom. Then she had helped Brent haul the rest of the stuff to the dump. She figured any furniture Brent had had to be better than what was there. The old sewing room had been converted into an office, as well as serving as storage space for the boxes of papers and photos Brent hadn't had time to go through yet.

Brent still hadn't touched the basement or the attic, but the house was looking one hundred percent better. Or at least it had been. Now it seemed that the only thing Brent had accomplished was to replace all of Levi's stuff with his own.

"Hey, Emma!" he called from somewhere inside the house. "Could you give Greg and Skip a hand in the living room?"

She stood up and poked her head into the front door. "Sure." Greg and Skip had to be the Incredible Hulk twins that had just disappeared into the back of the moving van. She lightly ran down the steps and hopped into the back of the van. The darn thing was still over half full. Greg and Skip each had an end of a midnight blue leather couch.

"What can I help you with, boys?" she asked. They looked like they could handle a mere couch, but sometimes furniture could be deceiving. The sucker could weigh two tons instead of just one.

Greg and Skip looked at each other, the massive couch between them, then at Emma. "We don't need you to help lift anything, Mrs. Haywood. We just need you to tell us where you want this."

"The name's Carson, not Haywood." She didn't like people jumping to the wrong conclusion about her relationship with Brent, even if it was the respectable assumption that they were married. The day before, when she had gone into town for a load of chicken feed, she had seen the looks a couple of town folks threw her way. Strawberry Ridge's tongues were wagging, she was sure of it. She looked at the couch. "You can put that in the empty living room." It shouldn't take a college education to figure that one out.

The muscles in Greg's arms bulged as he lifted his end of the couch. "We know it goes in the living room, Ms. Carson. But Mr. Haywood is paying us extra to set the furniture up. We need to know where in the living room you want it."

She felt like a heel as Greg and Skip maneuvered the sofa out of the truck, up the porch steps, and in through the doorway of the house. She had just taken out her frustration—with Brent for putting her in this situation and with the town for expanding the problem—on two innocent men. Here Greg and Skip expected her to stand in the middle of the living room directing them as to the proper furniture placement, as if she were Queen Elizabeth and this were Buckingham Palace. She knew zip about decorating, and the only guide she had about couches was that they had to be facing the television.

Emma jumped from the back of the truck and followed Greg and Skip into the house. She just hoped the television had already been set up.

Brent couldn't stand the laughter a moment longer. What were Greg, Skip, and Emma doing down there that was so hysterical? For the past hour, while he and Buzz had been setting up the bedroom, trying to make it sleepable for that night, the three amigos downstairs had been having a ball. It was a hard pill to swallow, but he had to admit, he was jealous. Emma never laughed like that with him.

He glanced at Buzz, who had just finished placing the last drawer into the dresser. "Why don't we go see how the others are doing?" The hose was connected from the bathroom sink to his water bed. It was going to take a while for the bed to fill up.

Buzz glanced at the pile of boxes stacked by the door and frowned. "You don't want me to help you unpack?"

"No, I can do that later." He walked out of the bedroom before Buzz could think of something else he could help with. The man seemed determined to work for every penny Brent was paying him.

Buzz stopped at the pile of boxes and the wicker hamper sitting outside the bathroom door. "What about all this bathroom stuff?"

"It's just towels and such. I'll unpack it all later," Brent said as he hurried down the steps. By the sound of it, Emma was having the time of her life, and he wasn't there.

He stopped at the bottom of the steps and glared into the living room. Emma was sitting in the middle of the couch with Greg and Skip on either side. All three were holding tall glasses of lemonade and laughing at something Emma had said.

"Is this the room the party's in?" He used the same tone of voice a parent would use if he arrived home unexpectedly and found his teenage daughter throwing a party in their home.

Greg and Skip immediately jumped up and looked chagrined. Emma patted the cushion next to her. "Sit here, Brent, and tell me what you think."

"Think about what?" He honestly didn't believe she wanted to know what he was thinking that very minute. He walked across the room and sat down beside her. The leather moaned under his weight.

"Put your feet up and relax. Pretend that you just came in from a hard day of cleaning chicken coops."

"Did I take a shower first?"

Emma wrinkled her nose. "I should hope so." She picked up his feet and placed them on the glass-and-brass coffee table in front of the couch. "There, now tell me what you see."

He looked around in confusion. What was he supposed to be looking for? He glanced over at Greg and Skip, who were shaking their heads and muttering something about Emma making them move it all again. "What am I supposed to be seeing?"

"The television, Brent. You're supposed to be watching the evening news."

He looked at the television in the far corner of the room and frowned. A person would have to be standing in the hall to see the screen clearly. "The news doesn't come on for another three hours, Emma."

"Brent, can you, or can you not, see the screen clearly?"

He moved closer to Emma and practically sat on her lap. "A person would need a periscope to see the blasted thing."

Greg and Skip groaned and buried their heads in their massive hands. Emma giggled, handed Brent her glass of lemonade, and stood up. "Well, boys, it's back to the old drawing board."

Brent sat there in amazement. Emma had actually giggled. He frowned at the grinning twins for having this strange power over his Emma. Taking a sip of her lemonade, he tried to cool down and ended up frowning deeper. Emma had made these massive hulks hand-squeezed lemonade when all he ever got was the granulated crystal kind. "What is it you want moved, Emma, and I'll move it." He could flex muscles with the best of them.

Buzz, Greg, and Skip all exchanged glances. Skip gave a slight sigh before speaking. "It's not that we don't want to move it all again, Mr. Haywood. We were just sharing a private joke with Emma."

"What do you mean by *all* again?" The living room now held the leather sofa and matching recliner, two wing chairs upholstered in a deep-blue-and-gold print, assorted glass-and-brass tables, lamps, an eight-by-five-foot area rug, a television complete with a VCR, and boxes filled with videotapes. In the far corner sat his pride and joy still unpacked, a stereo system that could shatter every window within a mile.

"Emma has had us move it, what?" Skip glanced at Greg and shrugged. "Eight times already."

Brent looked around the room. It looked fine to him. "What's wrong with the way it is?"

"Aren't you the one who just said you can't see the television without a periscope?" Emma asked. She glanced at Greg and Skip. "Come on, you two, it's grunting time again." She looked at Buzz. "Why don't you and Brent go ahead into the kitchen. There's a pitcher of fresh lemonade in the refrigerator and a plate full of cookies on the table. Help yourselves." She tapped the top of the television. "Okay, Greg, how about if we move it over this way another three feet."

"But what do we do with the chair that's there?" Skip asked.

"Damned if I know." Emma shook her head. "We'll find a place for it later."

"Isn't that what she said about the stereo, and it's still sitting in some corner?" Greg complained good-naturedly.

Brent stormed out of the room, calling to Buzz as he went. "Come on, let's get something cold to drink. Obviously we aren't needed here."

Emma looked at the empty doorway Buzz and Brent had just disappeared through and frowned. "Men. Go figure."

Two hours later Emma slapped a bowl of re-heated stew—left over from the previous night's dinner—in the center of Brent's oak kitchen table. Levi's old scarred and wobbly table and chairs had ended up on the front porch. "You were plain rude and impolite to the movers," she said to him. Brent's microwave sure made heating dinner a snap. Only catch was, she wasn't in the mood to eat after Brent had practically run Greg, Skip, and Buzz out of the house.

"You were about to invite them to dinner." Brent dumped a couple of spoonfuls of stew onto his plate.

"Why not? They seem like nice boys."

"Emma, they weren't boys, they were men." He stabbed at the butter and spread some across a roll.

"By the size of them, I don't think they were ever boys, even when they were."

In exasperation she shoved her plate to the side. She'd be the first one to admit she knew absolutely nothing when it came to the way a man thought. But Brent's recent behavior had pushed her limited boundaries to the max. "What is your problem?"

"My problem?" He shook his fork at her. "I wasn't the one giggling."

"Giggling?" Her voice squeaked in protest. "You acted like a rude, ill-mannered jackass in front of a bunch of fellow New Yorkers, who, I might add, were bending over backward to please you." She didn't add that she had been rearranging the living room over and over again just so she could get it perfect for him. She had wanted to show Brent she could do something as simple and feminine as arrange a living room. But she had failed even at that. Sure, you could see the television from the couch now, but one of the wing chairs had to be moved to the office and the entire room had an unbalanced look to it. "And now you have the audacity to say I was giggling." She stood up and glared across the table at him. Glaring was better than crying, and the tears were about to fall any second. "I'll have you know that I have never giggled in my life." She stormed into the mudroom and threw over her shoulder, "I'm going to check on *our* chickens. Enjoy your meal in solitary splendor." The slamming of the back door echoed her angry departure.

A half hour later Emma sat under the same maple tree where she had kissed Brent, and stared at the setting sun. The chickens were all secure in their runs for the night, and her tears had stopped falling. Now they were pooled behind her eyes, just waiting for the slightest provocation to overflow again. That was the reason she hadn't returned to the house. Brent was likely to provoke a waterfall tonight. She had never seen him like this before. He had always been courteous and polite to everyone, including that pushy truck salesman, Leon. So what had been his problem with Greg, Skip, and Buzz? They were just a bunch of friendly college students making some money on the side. They actually knew less about interior decorating than she did. And their charming antics had made her laugh, not giggle. Having some laughter in her life was as rare as love, and Brent had to go and ruin it.

She watched as he turned on a couple of lamps in the living room, flicked on the front porch light. That simple act of concern released a few more tears. Her own father had never left a porch light burning for her, and he was family. Brent, who'd been a stranger just weeks ago, had shown her more caring and respect than her entire family had in the eighteen years she had lived with them. Maybe she was being too harsh and judgmental of Brent. There had to be some reason behind his rudeness to the movers besides her laughter.

Emma rose to her feet, brushed off her bottom, and headed for that burning porch light and home.

❖━━━━━━━━━━❖

Brent looked up from the stereo he was connecting when Emma walked into the room. It had taken every ounce of willpower he possessed not to go after her before. The only thing that had kept him from going and looking for her when she didn't return was the fact that he was going to look awfully stupid when he tried to explain why he was jealous. Brent had never been jealous of anyone before in his life, and he didn't like the feeling now.

He involuntarily stared at her long bare legs. Silky tanned skin greeted his gaze from the top of her sneakers to the frayed edges of her denim cut-offs. No one looking at the old faded shorts and white T-shirt with a klutzy looking cartoon chicken printed across the front would consider the outfit sexy. Not until Emma put it on. Emma did more for cotton by just wearing it than Eli Whitney had ever done.

For weeks he had been the only one to see Emma in shorts. The view had been all his to savor and to fantasize about. His favorite fantasy had been wondering what those incredibly long limbs would feel like wrapped around his waist. That day, three handsome college boys had enjoyed the view and may have even contemplated the same fantasy. His reaction to the movers could have been classed as territorial, but he preferred to think of it as plain old jealousy. He didn't like other men looking at Emma's legs or any other part of her anatomy.

He set down the screwdriver he'd been using to assemble the shelving for the stereo, and smiled. "Hi."

Emma shuffled her feet and looked somewhere over his left shoulder. "Hi."

"I saved you some dinner. It's in the microwave." He didn't bother to tell her that after she'd left without touching her dinner, he hadn't be able to touch his. His plateful of stew had ended up in the garbage.

"Thanks." She moved a few more feet into the room. "Sorry for storming out of here like that."

Her apology made him feel even worse. What had she to be sorry about? He was the one who had acted like an idiot. He should be counting his blessings that she hadn't dumped the bowl of stew on his head. He slowly stood up. "I think I'm the one who should be apologizing."

Her eyebrows shot up in surprise, and she watched as he walked over to the couch and sat down. "Really?"

He noticed her shock and wondered how many people had ever apologized to Emma in her life, especially men. From what little she had told him about her father and brothers, he doubted very much that any of them had ever offered an apology. Levi would have just as soon ripped out his own tongue than utter an "I'm sorry." His own mother's and grandfather's relationship proved that point in spades. No, he doubted if Emma had ever received an apology. He patted the couch cushion next to him. "Sit down, partner, I think we may have a problem here."

She sat on the far end of the couch. "What problem?"

He frowned at the space between them, then said, "I was jealous."

Emma blinked twice and sputtered, "Jealous? Jealous of what?"

"Your laughter."

"My laughter?" It was her turn to frown.

"I've never heard you laugh before. There've been a couple of times when you've given this sarcastic chuckle, but you've never really laughed. The day I landed on my butt while cleaning out one of the coops, I could have sworn there was a certain gleam in your eyes, but you kept a straight face."

"You have no idea how hard that was, considering you were covered in mud, hay, feathers, and chicken sh—" She grinned. "Droppings."

"So why didn't you burst out laughing? I would have if the situation had been reversed."

"Maybe I didn't know how you would react if I went into a hysterical fit of laughter. You didn't look too happy sitting there with chicken droppings splattered all over your body."

"Didn't you ever laugh at something one of your brothers did?" He sensed she had been trained not to show her emotions.

"I only made that mistake once. Jimmie wasn't very cordial when he was sporting a hangover." She shuddered at the memory.

Brother Jimmie sounded as charming as her father. "So why were you laughing with Greg and Skip?"

"Because they happened to have been very nice guys who didn't seem to mind moving the same furniture around for over an hour."

"The room looks fine, Emma."

"If you hadn't shoved them out the door and on their way so fast, I would have had them move it all again."

"What's wrong with the way it is?" He had never noticed this domestic compulsion of Emma's to move furniture around. In fact, he had to pull opinions and ideas out of her concerning the other rooms of the house.

"Everything's at this end of the room." She waved her hand in front of her. "It looks like everything's sliding across the floor and will be going out the picture window any minute now." She glanced at the stereo spread out on the opposite end of the room. "I wanted it perfect for you."

"For me?"

"Who in the hell else would I want it perfect for?" she snapped. "It's the first thing you ever asked me to do, and I couldn't seem to get it right."

"It seems all right to me, and I've asked you to do plenty of stuff."

"You've asked me which color paint I prefer, or should you order sheers or lace curtains for the dining room, but you never asked me to handle an entire room. You said the living room was mine to

do with whatever I liked." She swiped at the tears
clinging to her lower lashes. "And I wanted to
make it perfect. I want to show you I'm quite capable of doing something besides caring for chickens,
tuning up tractors, and arguing with obnoxious
salesmen and getting you a better deal on that truck
you bought."

He moved closer and captured her hands. "No
one can argue about your expertise with chickens
or that tractor you're so fond of, Emma. As for the
money you saved me on the truck, I already told
you I have something special planned for that." He
squeezed her fingers and smiled. Emma had actually wanted to please him! "As for this room, it will
never be perfect with this furniture. This stuff"—
he gestured at the couch and chairs—"was purchased with my apartment in mind, not this room.
The pieces will never fit exactly."

"Great!" Emma cried as she snatched back her
hands. "All this time I was trying to do the impossible."

"What, fit all the furniture in?"

"No." She stood up and glowered at him.
"Please you."

Brent's heart jerked erratically as tears trickled
down her face. "Oh, Emma . . ." He stood and
cupped her chin so he could look into her eyes.
"Don't you realize how much you do please me?
That's the root of our problem." He captured a
tear with the tip of his finger. "I want you."

He saw the way her eyes widened and her lower

lip trembled, but she didn't say a word. "That's why I was jealous of Greg and Skip. They were looking at you with that interested gleam in their eyes."

"I'm four or five years older than them boys," she said. "You have to be mistaken, Brent. They were just being friendly."

His fingers brushed at the wisps of hair that had escaped her braid. "I ought to know when someone is interested in you, Emma. In fact, you could say I'm becoming quite an expert on the subject."

"Really?" Her gaze seemed riveted to his mouth.

"You have no idea how beautiful you are, do you?" His thumb stroked her cheek, brushing across a few wayward freckles the sun had brought out.

She shook her head, trying to deny what he was saying. "Brent, partners shouldn't lie."

"No, they shouldn't, Emma. That's why it's about time we got this out in the open." He took her hands and pulled her down on the couch with him. "What did you think all those silly I.O.U.'s were for?"

"Because you want to punish me."

He couldn't disguise the hurt in his voice. "Are my kisses that bad?" His expression turned pensive and he quickly released her hands. Maybe he had been wrong about Emma returning his interest. But how could he have misinterpreted her response?

She reached for his hands. "No, Brent, your kisses are wonderful and that's the punishment."

He turned his palms up and intertwined their fingers. "Now you've lost me. Explain how kissing me is punishment."

"Because we're partners." She shrugged and glanced away.

"What does us being partners have to do with us as a man and woman who find each other attractive?"

"It will only complicate matters, Brent," she whispered, and tried to dislodge her fingers from his grip.

"I'm willing to risk it, Emma. Are you?"

"I . . ." She bit her lower lip and stared down at their still-clasped hands.

"Something special happens when I kiss you, Emma." He raised one of his hands, still clasping hers, placed their combined fists below her chin, and raised her face. "Don't you feel it too?"

Her "Yes" was shaky and weak.

"I won't rush you, Em." He released her hand and, with his thumb, rubbed her lower lip where her teeth had left a faint mark. "We'll take it nice and slow." His tongue replaced his thumb with a sweet stroke. "Tell me you want to explore this feeling, Em."

"I do." She reached up and captured his mouth.

Brent moaned as pleasure exploded throughout his body. Emma wasn't going to hide from this attraction that thrived between them. She was going to give them a chance. He felt her melt into his embrace and deepened the kiss. He knew this wasn't a simple physical attraction he felt for Emma. It went deeper. It somehow connected with his soul, tore at his body, and obsessed his mind. His hands pulled her closer as he slanted his mouth across hers and plunged his tongue deep inside. He needed to taste every fiber of her sweetness.

Emma trembled and welcomed his onslaught. She pressed herself closer and they went down onto the couch in a tangle of arms, legs, and moans.

The more Brent's mind told him to slow down, the more impatient his hands became. When he pulled the hem of Emma's shirt from her shorts, she yanked his shirt from his. The hot patches of fire her fingers sparked as they brushed his bare side were igniting fires elsewhere. All below his waist. Within a heartbeat he was hard and aching. Never had he experienced such swiftness of desire. The feel of her bare legs tangled with his sent his resolve of slowness crashing. Smooth, silky skin brushed the coarse hairs covering his thighs. He wondered if she was that silky all the way up, and immediately his hands stroked her back.

The leather of the couch crinkled and moaned beneath their weight. The heat pulsating through her body echoed in her kiss.

Brent was on fire. He pulled his shirt over his head and dropped it to the floor. The moisture coating his bare back and legs was sticking to the leather. Smiling wickedly, he slowly pulled Emma's

T-shirt over her head. Two lacy cups overflowing with their treasures greeted his gaze. He looked up at her face. Not a speck of fear clouded her eyes, and she was smiling shyly. With a flick of his fingers he released the front clasp of her bra, and the twin mounds bounced free.

He tenderly cupped her breasts and held them higher for his inspection. "I told you you were beautiful." His thumbs rubbed across the rosy nipples, bringing them to harder peaks. "Now do you believe me?"

She arched her back, pushing her breasts into his palms. "Brent?" Her fingers wove through the dark curls covering his chest.

He raised his head and gently kissed each budding nub. "Hmmm?" They tasted like sweet wine and summer rain. They tasted like Emma.

She shook her head and whispered, "Nothing."

Brent felt the leather stick to his back and muttered a silent curse. This wasn't how he wanted to make love to Emma for the first time. Upstairs his king-size waterbed was filled and ready. Only problem was, he didn't think he had the strength or willpower to release Emma long enough to make it up those stairs. With a heavy shove of his foot he sent the glass coffee table skidding across the area rug. He held on to Emma as he rolled off the couch and onto the rug, carrying her with him. Next time, he promised himself, they would make it upstairs.

Emma felt the soft rug beneath her back and Brent's weight pressing down on top of her and willed herself to remain calm. This was Brent. She was safe. If she said no, he would stop. She shuddered as his mouth pulled on her breast and his hand stroked her side.

Brent gave the protruding nub one last lick and frowned. Something wasn't right. Emma's arms weren't around him any longer and she was lying beneath him like a stone. He raised his head in confusion. His bafflement lasted as long as it took for him to see the fear was back in her eyes. "Emma?"

"It's okay, I didn't say anything." Her voice sounded as if it was being pulled from her.

He rolled off her and sat up. "Tell me about it." He handed her her T-shirt.

"About what?" She sat up while clutching the cotton shirt against her breasts. The edge of the couch bit into her back.

"Tell me what put that fear back into your eyes." He raked a hand through his tousled hair and grabbed his shirt from behind him.

"What fear?" she asked. "I'm not afraid."

"Dammit, Emma, don't lie to me." He pulled his shirt over his head. "Partners shouldn't lie, remember." She looked so helpless and scared sitting there with her bra hanging open, her hair half unbraided, and her mouth swollen from his kisses. Lord, how he still wanted her. He hated to ask the next question, but he had to know. "Are you afraid of me?"

"No." She shook her head again, sending more

golden hair in every direction. The rubber band that had been holding the braid together was gone.

"Are you afraid of my touch?"

She lowered her eyes. "No."

"Then tell me what you're afraid of."

"I'm not afraid of you, Brent." She stood and dropped her shirt back onto the couch in a silent invitation.

Brent stood also, refusing to glance below her neck. If he did, he would be lost. Emma had been afraid, and was still fearing something, but what? "Emma, I'm going to ask you again. What are you afraid of?"

"I'm not afraid of anything, Brent."

She was lying. Emma was lying to him. He could see it in her eyes, see it in the way she held her trembling body. The crime of it was he still wanted her. He still wanted to make love to a woman who had nothing in her eyes but fear.

"I can't do it, Emma. I can't make love to you when all I see is your fear." He walked to the door and plucked his keys off the hook beside it. "The fear we could have worked out. But the lies, Emma . . . What did I ever do to deserve your lies?" With that, he walked out of the house, got into his truck, and drove away into the night.

EIGHT

Brent picked up the brown bottle of beer sitting in front of him, frowned, and placed it back onto the bar. The bottle was warm. Warm beer sounded about as appealing as Flo, the bleach-blond barmaid who had been giving him the come-on since he sat down. He wasn't in the mood for company or beer. For the past hour he had been sitting at the dark end of the bar in the only drinking establishment Strawberry Ridge had to offer, the Buds and Suds. The noise level had been steadily increasing since he'd arrived, and his thoughts hadn't had a chance to straighten themselves out.

Stopping in and having a few had seemed like a good idea when he'd passed the place after leaving Emma. Now he knew it wasn't. A person couldn't think straight with country songs and bluegrass music blaring out of the jukebox and a ball game blasting from the television behind the bar. A group of good ol' boys were arguing about something, and the cracking of pool balls shattered the noise about every thirty seconds.

He picked up the beer bottle again and set it back down without taking a sip. He shouldn't be there, surrounded by strangers. He should be home making love to Emma. Brent frowned as a group of locals moved down to his end of the bar, momentarily interrupting his thoughts of Emma. What had she been afraid of, and why would she lie about it? The fear only surfaced when they were kissing, but she didn't seem to be afraid of him as a person. So the fear had to be connected to the physical act of love. His heart missed the next two beats as ugly thoughts filtered through his brain.

Emma's childhood sounded about as loving as a concentration camp. Her father was a foulmouthed drunk, and her older brothers didn't appear to be pillars of the community. Acid scourged his gut as he wondered how abusive her home life had been. Her lying about not being afraid could have been out of shame, not deceit. Why in the hell had he left her standing in the middle of the living room looking so damn desirable and confused? He should have stayed and somehow made her talk. But if he had stayed, he would have accepted her silent invitation, carried her up to his bed, and regretted it in the morning. He had wanted Emma so badly, he had been on the verge of ignoring her fear. What kind of man did that make him?

The three men occupying the barstools next to

him seemed to be half loaded and begging for his attention. He glanced at them, didn't recognize any of them, and went back to contemplating his warm, half-drunk beer and mentally beating himself. Emma deserved someone who had a lot more self-control than that.

"So you're the city boy Emma's shacking up with."

Every muscle in Brent's body tightened as he slowly turned on the stool and studied the man sitting next to him. He appeared to be in his late twenties, and Brent imagined did construction work where he got to play the part of the bulldozer, and if the way his eyes seemed to have trouble focusing was any indication, he was drunk. "I'm Levi James's grandson and now Ms. Carson's *partner* in the farm, if that's what you were referring to." He knew the town was speculating on his relationship with Emma, but he didn't like this stranger's tone or attitude.

"Partnering," the man sputtered after taking a swig of beer. "Is that what you city folks call it nowadays?" The two men sitting next to him grinned and elbowed each other in the gut. "We still call it bagging around these parts."

Brent's fist tightened around his bottle. The man was asking for it. Brent had no idea who he was, or why he was being deliberately insulting, but he'd had about enough. Years of training from his mother and his former agent kept him sitting there looking nonchalant. Never get involved in a scandal. Brent wondered if smashing some jerk's teeth down his throat in a roadside dive would be considered a scandal. "Listen, buddy, I don't know who you are and I really don't care. I suggest you and your friends here go sleep it off someplace before I take offense."

"Guess he's been keeping company too long with all those chickens Emma's raising," joked the man farthest from Brent as the bar grew quiet. "He's starting to act like one, ain't he, Jack?"

The man beside Brent grinned widely and stuck out his hand toward Brent. "Name's Jack Roddman. Thought you might like to shake the hand of the man who broke the ground before you."

Brent stared at the outstretched hand. It seemed everyone in the bar was listening to this jerk and waiting for something. He had a sick feeling burning in his gut that had nothing to do with his lack of dinner. "What in the hell is that supposed to mean?"

"Sweet Emma Jane?" Jack raised a brow and grinned wider.

Brent's dark eyebrows met as he scowled. There was murmuring and muttering around him, but he ignored them all and concentrated on the man sitting on the next barstool. Rage, like none he had ever felt before, started to boil up inside him. "What about Emma?"

"Why, I'm the man who won a twenty-dollar bet the night I bagged her in the front seat of my pickup tru—" Brent's fist cut off anything else he would have said.

Brent watched as Jack fell backward off the stool and landed on his butt with a heavy thud. Fragments of teeth had flown out of his mouth along with a few drops of blood. Jack Roddman's boyish grin would never be the same.

Jack swiped at the blood flowing from his lip and stared in astonishment at Brent, still sitting on his barstool as if nothing had happened. With a vicious shake of his head he hauled his bulk off the floor and charged the man who had just embarrassed him in front of all his friends.

Brent barely had enough time to stand before the weight of the man carried them both back to the floor. Pain exploded in his jaw as Jack's fist connected. A couple of women screamed, and somewhere to his left a man was shouting encouragement to Jack. Brent ignored the yells and concentrated on getting to his feet and keeping out of the way of Jack's fist.

The two heaving men faced each other. Jack's lip was split wide open, and Brent could feel one of his eyes starting to swell shut. He gulped in some air and snarled, "That was for Emma." He couldn't believe it. This man had touched his Emma.

Jack spat a stream of blood onto the floor. "She wasn't worth no fat lip. All she did was cry and lay there like she was dead."

The rage churning inside Brent boiled over. With a shout of fury he charged Jack.

＊━━━━━━━━＊

Three hours later Brent sat on a lumpy cot in a jail cell, holding a cold rag to his face. Every bone in his body ached, his chest felt as if an elephant were sitting on it, his left eye was swollen shut, and the knuckles of his right hand were still oozing blood. He had just spent the last two hours being booked by the local sheriff for disorderly conduct, disturbing the peace, assault and battery, and destroying private property. It had been his bad luck that the owner of the Buds and Suds happened to be Jack Roddman's brother-in-law.

Still, Brent considered himself fortunate. Jack and his two buddies would have killed him if it hadn't have been for the help of his cell mate, Jimmie Carson, Emma's brother. When Brent had started to get the best of Jack, Jack's buddies had stepped in to help. Jimmie, who had been quietly observing the fight, hadn't liked the new odds and had proceeded to handle both of Jack's pals.

When the man who had helped him had been locked in the same cell, Brent had thanked him. That was when he discovered his comrade was Emma's brother. Jimmie had tried to smile around his fat lip and swollen jaw, saying it was no problem.

Brent glanced out of his right eye at Jimmie. He appeared to have gone to sleep on the other cot. How could the man sleep with the pain? Jimmie had to be hurting as much as he was. The sheriff had refused to give them so much as an aspirin until the local doctor arrived to check them out. Jimmie didn't look like Emma. Brent would have never guessed they were related. Jimmie was at least six foot three and had the build of an NFL linebacker and a head of thick dark-brown curls.

He didn't know what to make of the guy. Jimmie had barely spoken two words to him before falling asleep. Emma didn't seem to have any fond feelings toward her brothers, but Jimmie had come to Brent's aid while he was defending Emma.

Brent shuddered at the thought of Emma and Jack Roddman in the front seat of a pickup truck. Jack had said all she had done was lie there and cry. It sounded more like rape than romance. And it had been her first experience with a man. He now understood her fear.

He leaned back against the concrete wall and closed his eyes on the nasty scene he envisioned. He was sure Emma had wanted to make love with him that night, but her past kept rearing its ugly head. The denial of her fears had come from shame, not deceit. If Jack was positive he had been the first, it meant no one in her family had sexually abused her, which was what he had been beginning to think. It was Jack who had put the fear in her eyes. He should have done more than beat Jack senseless while he had the chance.

It was after two in the morning. He wondered if she was awake worrying about where he was, or if she'd gone to sleep. He wanted to rush home to her and tell her he now understood. All his life he had wanted someone to care for, someone to love. It looked as though he'd finally gotten his wish, and her name was Emma. When his fist had connected with Roddman's foul mouth, he had realized he was vindicating the woman he loved. Roddman deserved more than a fat lip and a black eye for what he did to Emma. Brent had always figured fighting was for uneducated brutes who didn't know any other way to settle disputes besides using their strength. He'd considered himself above that level, until tonight when Roddman had caught him off guard and demeaned Emma.

Since arriving in Strawberry Ridge, he had discovered many elements of himself he'd never known existed. He'd discovered who his grandparents had been, had cried for his sweet, loving grandmother, and he understood Levi's pain. He'd learned a lot about his mother's upbringing and was beginning to understand why she was the way she was. He'd also discovered he loved working outdoors, doing physical labor. At the end of each day, he looked at what he had accomplished and felt good about himself. When his grandfather had left him half of the Amazing Grace Farm, he'd also left him a chance to know Emma. Levi James had left his grandson his future.

Now all he needed to do was get out of jail and home to Emma so he could convince her to take a chance on him. Brent's gaze shot over to Jimmie, who was snoring lightly. Did Jimmie have someone worrying about him? Emma had never said if any of her brothers were married. Jimmie didn't have a wedding ring on his left hand, but that didn't mean there wasn't a wife somewhere.

"Hey, Haywood, doc's here to look at that eye." The sheriff unlocked the cell door and allowed a sleepy looking man dressed in wrinkled clothes and carrying a black bag to enter the cell. "As soon as he's done with you and Jimmie, you can make one phone call."

Brent glanced at Jimmie, who hadn't moved. "What about him?"

"Jimmie-boy?" The sheriff chuckled. "He ain't got no one to call who would give a damn if he lived or died, let alone pay his fine."

Brent sucked in a breath of pain as the doctor took away the damp rag and, none too gently, examined his sore eye.

Brent waited in dread for Emma to show up. She hadn't sounded too pleased when he'd called half an hour ago and asked her to bring the cash he had stashed in his sock drawer down to the sheriff's office. She also hadn't sounded as if he had awakened her, which could only mean she had been waiting up for him. It was a heck of a way to start a meaningful relationship. *Hey Emma, come bail me out of jail, and oh, by the way, I love you.* Brent shivered with distaste, gasped as pain shot through his ribs, and repositioned the ice bag the doctor had given him to help with the swelling closing his eye. By the feel of it, it was going to take an iceberg the size of the one that sank the *Titanic* to reduce the swelling.

"Hey, Haywood," the sheriff called, "you're free to go."

Brent slowly got to his feet, took a couple of shallow breaths, and pulled on his T-shirt to cover the mile of bandage the doctor had wrapped around his chest. He never knew a cracked rib could hurt so bad. With a last look at Jimmie, still snoring away, he walked out of the cell and into the outer office.

Emma was standing by the front window staring out into the night. She was wearing a pair of jeans and a clean black T-shirt, and her hair was loose and flowing down her back like a curtain of golden silk. By the stiff way she was holding herself, he could tell she wasn't thrilled to be there. "Em?"

She turned around, took one look at him, and rushed forward. "My God, Brent, what happened?" She reached to touch his face, but then stopped herself. "Who in the hell did this to you?" she demanded.

Brent tried to smile, but the movement caused more pain. Instead he tenderly brushed her pale cheek. Her freckles stood out against her pallor, and her eyes were red and puffy. "You've been crying."

She held his hand and studied the bandage

taped across his knuckles. "And you've been fight-ing."

He cringed at the disillusion laced into her ac-cusation. His fighting disappointed her. He didn't want to go into any details of the fight in front of the sheriff, so he simply shrugged.

Emma turned away as the sheriff said, "Sign here, Haywood, and you can go."

Brent turned to the sheriff and painfully signed where the man was pointing. "What's the bail for my cell mate?"

"There's no bail for him. Only a two-hundred-dollar fine for disturbing the peace."

Brent walked over to Emma. "Can I have the money, Em?"

"I already posted the bail." She reached in the pocket of her jeans and handed Brent the remain-ing bills.

He counted out two hundred dollars and jammed the rest into his pocket. "I know, thanks." The least he could do for Jimmie was pay his fine. He handed the sheriff the money and watched as he disappeared into the back where the cells were. He wasn't looking forward to Emma's reaction to his cell mate.

Emma went back to staring out into the night. Main Street through Strawberry Ridge was de-serted at three o'clock in the morning. She hadn't passed a soul on her way into town. After Brent had walked out on her earlier, she had gone upstairs, thrown herself across her bed, and cried. She hadn't meant to lie to Brent, but the truth was too painful to tell.

When the phone had rung after two A.M. her first thought had been, Brent had been in an accident. She'd been relieved to hear his voice, but when he had asked her to come into town to the sheriff's office and bring his money for bail, her heart had broken. Brent, the man she had thought was so different from every other man she knew, wasn't. He was the same as her father and brothers. There was only one place in the entire town of Strawberry Ridge where he could have found trouble at that hour of the morning, the Buds and Suds. The Carsons held the town record for the most arrests while patronizing the bar. It now appeared Brent wanted to give her family a run for their money. She gave a sad chuckle. At least Brent had the money to bail himself out. Her brothers never did.

She glanced away from the empty street, turning around as the sheriff and the man whose fine Brent had just paid entered the room. If she thought the shock of seeing Brent's face discolored and swollen had been bad, it was nothing compared to the shock she was receiving now seeing her brother, in the same condition as Brent, walk into the room. "Jimmie!"

Jimmie glanced between Brent and Emma. He gave a small shrug and said, "Hi, sis."

She looked at his right hand, noticed the split knuckles, and sputtered in outrage, "You did this"

—she waved her hand toward Brent's face—"to Brent?"

"No," Jimmie said as he took his wallet and other personal effects the sheriff handed him.

"Emma, calm down," Brent said as he placed his hand on her shoulder. She shrugged it off. "Your brother helped me."

"Jimmie?" Emma gave a sarcastic laugh. "Jimmie never helped another soul in his life."

"Maybe if you had bothered to come around in the past seven years," Jimmie said, "you would have noticed that some people do change." He jammed his keys into the front pocket of his jeans, winced at the pain that simple movement caused him, and walked over to the front door with barely a limp. "There's a saying, Emma, 'Better late than never.'" He looked away from his sister and toward Brent. "Thanks, Haywood. I owe you one."

"Consider it even," Brent said as Jimmie opened the door and disappeared into the night.

"What do you mean, he helped you?" Emma asked.

"When the odds started to stack against me, your brother stepped in and evened them out." Brent looked at the sheriff. "Is there anything else?"

"Just don't leave town unexpectedly."

Emma frowned at the sheriff's threatening tone of voice. Frank Roddman was usually a very even tempered and happy-go-lucky kind of guy. The only time she had seen him act nasty and use the badge pinned to his chest to his own advantage was when someone threatened his family, and that included his boastful, disgusting, and conceited nephew, Jack. Frank had a blind spot as large as the moon where his nephew was concerned. A sick feeling started to twist her stomach as she left the sheriff's office.

She stopped in front of old Betsy. "I'll drive you home. You aren't in any condition to be driving. If you're feeling up to it, we'll pick up your truck tomorrow."

Brent climbed into the passenger side of the truck without saying a word.

Emma noticed his sharp intake of breath every time she hit a pothole or bump. She tried to be more careful, but considering Betsy had rusty cylinders where shocks should have been, the going wasn't easy. They were over halfway home and the silence was killing her. Why didn't Brent say something, anything? "So, killer, how does the other guy look?"

Brent continued to stare out the windshield into the darkness. "Not nearly as bad as I would like him to."

"Going to tell me about it?" Her teeth worried her lower lip as she slowed down and maneuvered around another pothole.

"Not when my mind is clouded by pain and the effects of some pills the doctor gave me."

"What pills?" She didn't like the sound of his voice. His speech was slow and slurring.

He reached into the front pocket of his jeans and handed her a small white packet of pills. "Two every six hours, until I can stand the pain, then cut it back to one." He leaned his head back against the ripped vinyl of the seat and promptly fell asleep.

Three days later Emma frowned across the cornfield as she watched Brent make his way into a chicken run carrying a fifty-pound bag of feed. The man should be in bed still, not doing chores. That morning when she arrived downstairs for breakfast, she had been surprised to see Brent already there, ready to start the day. It seemed two days of bed rest had been sufficient time for him to recover. Most of the swelling in his face was down, though he sported more colors than a crayon factory.

It was getting to be late afternoon and he was just finishing what should have taken him only a few hours to do, and the packet of little white pills had been untouched all day. At lunch when she had reminded him to take one, he'd refused, saying they made his mind all fuzzy. Emma was unsure if it had been the effects of the pills or whoever he'd connected with down at the Buds and Suds that had scrambled his brains.

Brent hadn't brought up the subject of that night, and neither had she. She didn't know if she wanted to hear what had happened. The day after the fight, Jimmie had showed up at the farm and offered her a ride into town to pick up Brent's truck. She'd accepted the offer only because she knew what Brent had just paid for the truck and she had been curious as to why her brother would help Brent out in a fight. Jimmie, though, wouldn't discuss the fight or Brent. He contributed a total of three sentences to the conversation, all concerning the current heat wave. Emma had been dropped off in the Buds and Suds parking lot more confused than ever. The lift had been the second nice thing Jimmie had done for her in forty-eight hours. He had broken his lifelong record of good deeds, and it hadn't even started to snow.

Emma gave the waist-high corn one last look before heading back to the house to start dinner. If it didn't rain soon, there was a good chance they would lose the entire crop and with it any hope of expanding. Brent's pockets had to have a bottom somewhere. Once he saw how chancy farming was, he wouldn't bother to sink his nest egg into chickens and fate.

A few days later Emma regretted ever praying for rain. Since the afternoon she'd started to fear for the corn crop, it had rained steadily. The weatherman had forecasted rain in Missouri, not Arkansas. But Arkansas had received that storm and the three that followed. She was sick of the mud, wet clothes sticking to her body, witless chickens, and Brent's mood.

The man was driving her crazy without even

trying. His gorgeous face looked a hundred percent better. His lip had healed, his left eye was now only a strange shade of yellow, and he had stopped wrapping his ribs. He was back to doing all his work, but she had noticed that he sometimes flinched when picking up something heavy or when he accidentally bumped his ribs. He seemed to be waiting for something. What, she wasn't sure, and that was driving her crazy.

She finished drying the dinner dishes and wiping down the counters and table. The sound of the rain hitting the roof was grating on her nerves. She was beginning to feel like a prisoner in her own home. How could it continue to rain day after day without them all floating away? The Strawberry River was already overflowing its banks, causing some damage to low-lying farms. The Amazing Grace Farm was well out of danger, unless Crazy Pete's prediction came true. That morning when she had braved the storm to run into the feed mill for a few more bags of feed, she had heard the rumor that Crazy Pete was building an ark in his barn. Emma walked over to the mudroom windows and stared out into the swamp that had been the backyard. Maybe Crazy Pete knew something they didn't.

"See anything interesting?" Brent asked as he walked into the kitchen.

"Just more rain." She leaned her head against the cool glass for a moment before returning to the kitchen. "Weatherman said there's a cold front pushing its way through Missouri and all this should be cleared out of here by morning."

"Is the corn going to be all right?"

"If the rain stops within the next day or so, it should be fine. Right now it's a little soggy, but let the sun come out and you'll be able to hear it grow."

Brent chuckled. "Can you really hear it grow, or is that a hayseed joke?" He reached for the coffeepot and poured himself another cup.

"On summer nights when the air is still, you can hear the leaves rub against each other as they grow." *My God!* she thought. *We're talking like some old married couple about the weather and crops.*

"And the chickens?"

"They might rub up against one another, but you can't hear them grow." She raised a brow and waited for his comment on her smart mouth. She didn't want to discuss the corn, the rain, or brainless chickens. She wanted to know what the hell had happened at the Buds and Suds that night.

"I was referring to their health in all this rain, not their growth." He leaned against the counter and took a sip from his cup.

"Maybe you should be more concerned about your own health than the well-being of a bunch of brainless creatures who at least have the sense to get out of the rain and stay in their coops." He could have been seriously injured fighting in the Buds and Suds. Lord knows, she had seen her brothers come home in worse shape than Brent.

She had also seen their scars. If Brent ever wanted to get back into modeling, barroom scars would definitely be a liability. Never mind that to leave a mark on a man as beautiful as Brent would be sacrilegious.

He glanced around the kitchen. "Emma, I am out of the rain, nor do I go around standing in it for no purpose." He set his cup down on the counter. "Why don't you tell me what's really bothering you?"

"Bothering me?" She nearly choked on her astonishment.

"You're the one who's been pacing around the house like a tiger caught in a cage for days."

She scowled at his colorful eye. "I'm not the one starting barroom brawls."

"I didn't start it. I just finished it."

"Well, who the hell started it, and why did you sink to their level?" She shook her head in defeat. "I thought you were different."

"Different from whom?"

"All the men I've ever known." She willed the tears that were welling up to go away. Tears never solved anything. She'd promised herself when Brent walked out that night she would never lie to him again. No matter how painful the truth was. "I thought you were someone special." He might not want her because of her lies and fears, but she still wanted him. Brent Haywood was the best thing ever to happen to her, and it was disheartening to realize he was just human after all. She pulled out a chair and sat down. "I had you standing so high up on a pedestal that no one in Strawberry Ridge could touch you." She glanced at his eye again and managed a small smile. "It was a hell of a fall, wasn't it?"

He took the chair next to her and reached for her hand. "I'm glad I fell, Em." He squeezed her fingers. "I never asked to be put up there in the first place. I'm only a man."

"A man who likes to have his face used for a punching bag?"

"Considering that was my first fight, I think I did pretty well."

She believed him. In a strange way, Brent actually seemed pleased with himself. "Well, who did you fight, and I'll tell you if you fought the town's weenie or the town's bad boy."

His gaze locked on her face. "Jack Roddman."

Emma turned pure white before a wave of red swept up her face. *Jack Roddman!* She now understood the sick feeling in her gut when the sheriff had acted so hostile to Brent. "What did he do that provoked you enough to hit him?"

"He didn't do anything, it was what he said." His fingers stayed clamped around her trembling hand as she tried to pull it away.

With a sense of anxiety she quietly asked, "What did he say?"

Brent tightened his hold. "His exact words were that he had won a twenty-dollar bet the night he bagged you in the front seat of his pickup truck."

NINE

The tide of red that had swept up Emma's face completely disappeared. She now looked as if she had seen a ghost. Brent felt his heart jerk in his chest. He should have been more tactful with Emma and sugarcoated the truth, but he knew he couldn't. How could he expect the truth from her without giving her the same?

She closed her eyes and turned her head away. "You shouldn't have fought him, Brent. He was only telling the truth."

Brent frowned at the meekness in her voice. Since when had his Emma become so docile? "The truth has many sides, Em. I want to hear your side."

"Why, so you can know how easy I was?" She pulled her hand out of his grasp and glared across the table at him.

"No, so I can figure out how I'm going to kill

the son of a bitch." He took a deep breath and shook off the rage threatening to engulf him. He couldn't afford to give in to that rage, which had been simmering beneath his calm appearance for days. Emma needed his strength and understanding if she was going to face her fears. "That was uncalled for, Em, I'm sorry."

She gave a weak chuckle. "That depends on how you look at it."

"How do you look at it, Em?"

"I got what I asked for, Brent. Let's leave it at that."

"We can't leave it at that. Whatever happened is still affecting you. Can't you see how it comes between us?"

"So ignore it, Brent. I do."

"No, you don't, Em." He reached out and lightly caressed her hand, which was clenched into a fist on top of the table. "Don't you trust me?"

"Of course I trust you." Her gaze followed his finger as it outlined a blue vein across the back of her hand. "Maybe I don't want you to despise me."

"I could never despise you." He gave her a soft smile. "Trust me, Em."

She kept her gaze lowered. "In high school I wasn't the most popular girl." Her brow wrinkled with the painful memories. "In fact, I wasn't popular at all. I never dressed in the latest fashions; I was never invited to any parties or group gatherings. If I had been, I couldn't have gone anyway. I was too busy cooking and cleaning for my father and brothers. It took everything I had just to keep my grades up enough to graduate. I didn't have time for boys, and they surely didn't have time for me."

He could picture her growing up, alone, confused, and ignored. His rage shifted from Roddman to her family. Hadn't anyone seen what was happening? Hadn't they cared? "It must have been lonely."

She shrugged. "I lived." She started to worry her lower lip with her teeth as she searched for words. "I noticed boys, even if they ignored me. By twelfth grade I joined every other female in the school and was madly in love with Jack Roddman. He was the captain of the football team, the best-looking boy in the school, had his own pickup, and twice he smiled at me in the halls. Later I found out he had a cruel streak and was spoiled rotten. Anything Jack wanted, Jack got."

"He was your boyfriend?" He couldn't imagine Emma dating such a jerk. But then again she had only been seventeen. In his youth he had done some things that seemed questionable to him now.

"Lord, no. Jack didn't have one steady girl. He played the field, as they say, and every girl he looked at thought she would be the one to capture his heart. I wasn't immune to his charms. After graduation ceremonies a bunch of the more rowdy kids were going celebrating down by the dump. I was just leaving the school when Jack pulled up in his pickup and asked me if I wanted to go. You might have thought he'd offered me a million dollars, considering how fast I climbed up into the truck with him. I just knew I was going to be the one to win his heart. After all, it was my lucky day. I'd graduated from high school and was now free to leave home and go my own way."

Brent waited for Emma to continue, but she didn't. All she did was stare down at the table. "What happened?"

"The party had more beer than the Buds and Suds, and Jack made sure my cup was never empty."

Brent swore softly.

"He didn't force me to drink any of it, Brent. I willingly and knowingly drank every drop. I was having the time of my life. I was with the boy of my dreams, and I was at the party of the year. A couple hours later Jack wanted to leave the party and go somewhere quiet. We ended up parking on some deserted dirt road five miles from town. At first his kisses and caresses were great. This was what I had been missing all through school. This was Jack. I was the luckiest girl in the world." She glanced up and gave Brent a halfhearted smile. "Right?"

Brent felt sick to his stomach. He knew how this was going to end. Roddman deserved to be strung up. He wanted to pull Emma into his arms and never let her go, but she didn't look as though she was going to accept any comfort from him.

"Emma, you don't have to continue, I get the picture."

"You wanted the truth, so listen to it." Her hands rubbed her thighs. "At first I liked his kisses. Hell, I even participated in them. When things started to get out of hand and my beer-fogged brain started to clear, I said no." She gave a slight shudder and refused to meet his gaze. "Jack kept going. He took what had been offered."

"The son of a bitch is going to die!" Bone-chilling rage boiled over in Brent. He was going to take Jack apart, piece by piece.

"He only took what any other man would have," Emma said quietly.

"You said no. He should have stopped then and there with no questions asked." Brent couldn't believe she was actually defending the creep. "What he did has a name, Emma. It's called rape."

"It was my own stupid fault. I allowed him to take me parking. I was the one who drank and permitted his kisses." She stood up and cried, "I was the one who led him on."

"You were the one who also said *no.*" She wasn't defending the jerk, he realized, she was taking the blame. Oh, Lord, how could she even think it was her fault? He stood up and took a step toward her. "Emma, Roddman was in the wrong. What he did was a crime. He should have been reported to the sheriff."

"Oh, that would have been cute. Me, a white-trash Carson, go waltzing into Jack's uncle's office and explaining how his precious nephew, the pride of Strawberry Ridge High, hadn't taken no for an answer." She turned her back and gripped the edge of the sink. "The only thing that happened was what is supposed to happen between a man and a woman."

Brent's heart constricted more. The sheriff being Jack's uncle explained a lot. Like why Jack hadn't been arrested that night at the Buds and Suds, and why the sheriff hadn't treated Brent or Jimmie very cordially while they were visiting his jail. "You're wrong, Em." He turned her around and shuddered at the look on her face. She looked broken by the memories. "What Jack did was a violent act. It has nothing to do with what happens between a man and woman when they care about each other."

Her lip looked sore and tender from where she had been chewing on it. She raised her tear-filled eyes and softly asked, "Do you care about me?"

Care about you! Hell, I'm in love with you. He didn't think this was the time to share that piece of news. She looked so damn vulnerable and unsure of herself. He reached out and wiped a single tear from her cheek. "Very much, Em."

She seemed to search his face for a long time before whispering, "Show me how it should be between a man and a woman."

Brent closed his eyes and willed his heart not to

explode with joy. Just knowing that she trusted him enough to suggest such a thing should be a victory. "Oh, Em." The back of his fingers caressed the gentle slope of her jaw. "Don't tempt me with such a sweet offer."

The hope faded from her eyes. "You don't want me?" She tried to take a step back, but only ended up bumping into the counter.

"I want you more than my next breath."

"But?"

"I can't take advantage of you, Em." He kept plenty of distance between them and tried not to crowd her. "You just suffered a shock."

"What shock?"

"You just relived a horrible experience!"

"I've lived with it for seven years, Brent. I don't think I'll go into shock tonight." The tears had stopped flowing, and hope was beginning to sparkle once again in her eyes. "I got a little weepy tonight because I never told anyone about it, that's all."

He noticed the way her shoulders straightened and her chin rose. His Emma was back. This wasn't going at all the way he'd envisioned it. Shouldn't he be comforting her instead of fantasizing about her long, smooth legs and the sweetness of her mouth? Desperate for something to say, something to take their minds off what she had just suggested, he blurted out, "Why don't we have dessert?"

Emma smiled, really smiled for the first time in days. Brent was unsure of himself, she realized. He wanted her, she could tell by the bulge threatening the zipper on his jeans, but his conscience was trying to override his hormones. The hell with his misplaced principles, she thought. She wanted to experience all the wonders his kisses had promised. She had told him the truth: She wasn't upset or traumatized after telling him what had happened. He hadn't looked at her accusingly or with blame as she had once feared. He didn't despise her for what had happened. It was awfully sweet of him to be so thoughtful and considerate, but totally unnecessary. As he had said, that wasn't how it was between a man and a woman who cared about each other, and she believed him. She wanted to experience all the joy and wonder with him.

A small ember of confidence in herself as a woman sparked. She had seen the way other woman looked at Brent, as if he were a juicy side of beef and they had been on a vegetarian diet for too long. She had also noticed that Brent didn't pay any attention to their drooling. With his looks and charm he could probably have any woman under the age of sixty in the entire state, yet he'd chosen her and a rundown chicken farm for company.

She took a step closer to him and secretly smiled at the way he stiffened. With a gentle touch she straightened the collar on his polo shirt. "Are you sure it's dessert you want?"

He swallowed hard as her hand caressed his chest in a slow downward movement. "Emma, think real carefully before you move that hand another inch."

She gave him a wicked smile and slid her fingers down another three inches. "Brent?"

"What?"

His voice had the deep, raspy sound of desire. "I'm not saying no."

He captured her hand before it traveled any farther. "You can say no anytime, and I'll stop without a protest."

"I know." She brought his hand up to her mouth and kissed the faded cut across the knuckles. He had suffered all that pain because he had defended her. She felt humble and exhilarated at the same time. No one had ever stood up for her before. She was planning on kissing every one of Brent's wounds and making the hurt go away.

She tugged on his hand and started to lead him out of the kitchen and up the stairs. Smiling shyly, she admitted, "I've never slept on a waterbed before."

"Emma, I've got news for you." Brent gave her his melt-your-knees grin as he allowed her to pull him up the stairs. "We're not going to get much sleep tonight."

She blushed a brilliant scarlet but continued to lead the way. Her feet faltered momentarily when she entered the master bedroom and looked around. It looked the same as it did every time she passed the room and glanced inside. The king-size waterbed, draped in a silver and black spread, looked to be roughly the size of her entire bedroom. How did he sleep in it without getting lost? The matching furniture was all clean lines and modern. He had painted the room a pale gray, the oak floor gleamed from several coats of varnish, and the windows were bare except for shades. His redecorating of the house had been delayed due to his injuries.

He squeezed her hand and studied her face. "Change your mind?"

"No." She nodded toward the bed. "Just wondering if I should ask for a life preserver first."

He took her hands and placed them on his chest as he pulled her closer. "You could always hang on to me. I'm an excellent"—he glanced at the bed and grinned—"swimmer."

Emma moved her hands up and encircled his neck. The heated look in his eyes promised a slow trip to heaven. She didn't want slow, however. She wanted heaven, and she wanted it now. It had taken her seven long years to find a man she could trust enough to take her on that journey. She wasn't about to wait a moment longer. She pressed herself against his body and grinned back. "You don't say?"

Brent's mouth captured her grin. His hands pulled her closer as he parted her lips with a sweep of his tongue.

Heat rushed through her body as she greeted his kiss with a demand of her own. She didn't want

Brent being wary or cautious with her. Her teeth tenderly caught his lower lip as her tongue stroked its fullness. When she felt the tremble that shook his body, she released his mouth and trailed tiny kisses up his jaw to the corner of his eye. She softly kissed the discolored skin.

Brent's hands slid under her shirt and rubbed tantalizing circles across her back. His legs parted and he pulled her closer still. "Em, we have to slow down."

She continued to cover his face with kisses, exploring the plane of his nose, his jaw where the roughness of his beard tingled against her lips, and the indentation where a dimple appeared whenever he smiled. Her hands greedily pulled the shirt from his pants before stroking up his back. "Why?"

Her shirt was yanked over her head and tossed aside. "Because I want you to relax and enjoy this."

With impatient hands she pulled his shirt over his head. "Do I look uptight to you?" Her mouth gently pressed against the sore rib before skimming its way up to his throat. She could feel the rapid pounding of his heart beneath her lips.

Her bra landed on the oak floor, and her breasts overflowed his hands. He placed a kiss on each nipple before raising his head. "I want to be able to see your eyes, Em."

"Why? They're just blue."

"No, they aren't." He caressed her cheek. "The other morning, before all this rain, the sky was exactly the same color as your eyes." He leaned forward and kissed the lid of each eye. "You have gorgeous eyes, and they can't hide your fear, Em. I need to know if I do something wrong, or if I hurt you."

"Don't put on the kid gloves and treat me like some invalid, Brent." She held his callused palm to her cheek and rubbed against it. "Treat me like a woman."

He shuddered, cupped both her cheeks, and kissed her deeply. "All right, Em, if you promise not to hide your fear."

Her "I promise" was whispered against his neck as he swept her up into his arms and carried her to the bed. The satin spread cooled her back as he laid her down in the middle of the bed. Her body rocked for a moment as he lay down beside her and pulled her against his chest. Liquid heat gushed to the junction of her thighs, coating the walls of her womanhood with moist acceptance. Her breasts grew heavy and her nipples hardened into tiny pebbles as they rubbed against the soft curls blanketing his chest.

Brent's hands squeezed and pressed her rounded bottom as his hips arched upward, allowing her to feel his arousal beneath his jeans. He reached for her mouth and kissed her deeply as she pressed herself closer to his straining need. His fingers toyed with the snap on her jeans as he broke the kiss and gazed into her eyes.

Emma smiled knowingly. There wasn't any fear for him to see. "It's all right, Brent. I want you."

He matched her smile with a larger grin as her fingers duplicated every move his made. When he lowered her zipper, she lowered his. When he gave her jeans a tug down her hips, she tugged his. With playful banter the rest of their clothes were removed in a hurry.

Emma gloried in the kaleidoscope of feelings rocketing through her. Strange but delicious sensations tingled deep inside while hot flames danced across her skin wherever Brent touched. His hands were gentle yet commanding in their exploration of her body. She returned the favor with nimble fingers stroking the many textures of his body. The smooth leanness of his hip, the hair that covered his thighs, the solid wall of his chest. Her confidence and excitement expanded with every shudder of his body. Brent was feeling everything she was.

Her breath lodged in her throat as his fingers swirled their way up the inside of her thigh. Reaching higher. She shivered as he brushed the dark golden curls screening the slick walls of her desire, then groaned in frustration when he stopped. She instinctively jerked her hips upward, silently pleading with him.

Brent watched her eyes as he wove his fingers through the thick curls and slipped one inside the tight moist opening. He closed his eyes and moaned as her sweetness constricted around him.

Emma arched her hips higher off the bed and rolled her head from side to side. She trembled with need as Brent kissed the tip of each breast and inserted a second finger. He was still lying beside her on his side. His hard, jutting shaft nudged her thigh as his fingers plunged and retreated, only to plunge again. A coil of need twisted and tightened deep within her, matching the rhythmic motion of his hand. She could feel the coil ready to snap and gasped his name.

He slowly removed his fingers and kissed her lips. "This is where you have to tell me no, Em. Before it's too late."

She shook her head, clutched his hip, and tried to pull him on top of her. He didn't budge. "Brent?"

"Tell me this is what you want." His fingers brushed a tangled golden curl off her cheek.

"This is what I want." She slid her hand down his chest and circled the nest of dark curls at the base of his shaft. Desires she didn't fully understand thickened her voice. "You are what I want." She arched her hips against the emptiness he'd left behind. "Make the ache go away, please."

Brent groaned a feverish prayer and closed his eyes for a second before rolling over and reaching into the nightstand drawer for a red foil package.

Emma watched entranced as he rolled the prophylactic into place with shaky fingers. Not only did the simple act drive the ache inside her to a feverish pitch, but it was also the sweetest, most caring gesture he could have made. It showed exactly how much he cared. She reached out and hesitantly touched the tip of his shaft. The pulsating muscle jerked beneath her finger. With three older brothers and her ordeal with Jack, she wasn't totally ignorant of the male body. Logic and experience told her she should be afraid of the hard shaft, but one look at the strain on Brent's face convinced her he was in pain. "Does it hurt?"

He reached up and pulled her head down to his. "It's the sweetest pain known to man." He held her mouth in a kiss born of desire and need as he lifted her onto his rock-hard body. His arousal teased the moist curls between her thighs, and he rocked her back and forth without releasing her mouth.

Emma moaned and tried to fill the ache inside her with his strength. She broke the kiss, spread her thighs farther apart, and straddled his hips. The feel of his arousal nudging her center caused her to smile. Brent was allowing her to set the pace and to command the dominating position. His reasons were obvious and her heart cried out in joy at the thoughtfulness behind the gesture.

She tilted her head back as his fingers stroked up the inside of her thighs to the silky slick opening. With the gentlest of touches, he brought her to new heights while slowly filling her with his shaft. When he was completely inside, she closed her eyes and smiled at the sensation. It was tight, hot, and oh so heavenly. She moved her hips and was rewarded with new sensations and Brent's curse.

"Don't move!" He held her hips still and closed his eyes.

"Why?"

"You need time to adjust." He took slow, steady breaths.

It hadn't hurt her. In fact, it felt sinfully good. "Brent?" She rolled her hips again and was encouraged by his groan of pleasure. "I think I've adjusted." Her hips moved once more as his hands started to rock them into a rhythmic dance. The coil deep inside her immediately tightened, and her body found the natural rhythm between a man and a woman. His hands stroked up her rib cage to squeeze her swaying breasts and teasingly pinch the hard nipples.

The coil tightened even more, and Emma rocked harder. She didn't understand where she was going, she only knew she had to get there, and Brent was the one to take her. She cried out his name as his fingers stroked down her abdomen, through the nest of curls, and grazed the throbbing nub between her thighs. The coil shattered into a million fragments of release. Every fiber of her body released its hold on her soul and freely floated.

Emma felt Brent plunge upward one last time before shouting her name and pulling her down onto his chest. His heavy breaths disturbed her hair, and his fingers clutched at her hips. He seemed to be having the same experience she had gone through.

She tried to smile against his chest, but she was still trembling too much from the aftershocks. All she could manage was a shaky "Oh my God."

Brent pulled her closer and whispered, "You can say that again."

He was still deep inside her, filling her completely with his velvety strength. She raised her head, glanced at his perspiration-soaked face, and said, "Oh my God."

TEN

Emma stopped in the hallway before entering the kitchen the next morning. She was trying to decide what was the proper etiquette for the morning after. Her experience on such matters rated up there with playing golf, a big fat zip. She had seen the scene played out dozens of times on television, but seeing it and doing it were two entirely different things. First, she didn't own a silky robe to go slinking across the kitchen in. And second, after last night, she didn't think Brent could have any energy left for serving her what she considered a "start your morning" kind of breakfast. The man had been phenomenal last night. If she had a rooster in the henhouse with as much stamina as Brent, she could double their productivity and own the only grinning hens in Arkansas.

She glanced down at herself and shook her head. She was acting as silly as those grinning hens.

After waking alone in his bed, she had taken a long
hot shower to relieve some of the delicious soreness
in muscles she'd never known she possessed. Then
she had done something totally out of character.
She had stood in the middle of her bedroom for ten
minutes trying to decide what to wear. She'd ended
up pulling on a pair of khaki shorts that had been
gathering dust in her closet and a brand-new white
T-shirt. High fashion it wasn't, but it was a lot better than some of the outfits she'd worn around
Brent. She had even pulled on the new boots she
had picked up the week before while in town with
Brent. They were a cross between a construction
boot and a hiking boot, and Brent had laughed
himself silly when he'd found her in the boys' shoe
department trying them on. They would probably
be ruined by the mud outside, but she wanted to
look her best this morning, and this was the *best* she
got.

It was plain, simple vanity that had made her
pull on the lacy white panties and bra and braid her
hair twice. The first braid had seemed too strict and
tight; she had softened and loosened it the second
time. She was tempted for a full five seconds to try
the free sample of perfume she had gotten about six
months earlier in the mail, but common sense had
prevailed. Every insect this side of the Strawberry
River would sniff out the flowery scent and come
a-calling. Swiping at mosquitoes the size of an air-
craft all day wasn't what she considered fun.

Her neat, clean appearance was the only way

she knew to hide her insecurities about facing Brent that morning. All three times they had made love the night before, the light had been on. She had a feeling Brent had purposely left it on so she wouldn't be frightened. Just like his reasons for taking the bottom twice and then, amazingly, making love to her while they were both on their sides. She hadn't been afraid. In fact, she had been quite eager for his touch. There was no way she could compare what had transpired between them last night and what had happened seven years ago with Jack Roddman in the cramped front seat of his truck. Facing Brent this morning over breakfast was still going to be difficult, though. She didn't know what to say, or how to act. Would it be proper to mention it at all? Did she pretend the whole night had never happened, or grovel at his feet, profusely thanking him for sharing his expertise in such a manner?

The smell of freshly brewed coffee and sizzling bacon finally drew her into the kitchen. Her mind might not be ready to face Brent, but her stomach was. He was standing in front of the stove, turning sizzling strips of bacon and keeping an eye on a pan full of eggs. The table was already set for two, complete with orange juice and a vase containing a colorful assortment of weeds and flowers that grew around the house. Brent had been one busy man that morning.

She stopped about a foot behind him and glanced over his shoulder at the scrambled eggs bubbling away. "Good morning." It sounded inept to greet your lover with a friendly "good morning," but she figured it beat a sloppier gush of gratitude.

Brent finished flipping the last piece of bacon, turned around, and swept her up into a tight hug. His mouth swooped down on hers with more sizzle than the bacon. When he finally broke the kiss, he cleared his throat and grinned. "Good morning to you too."

She grinned back. "I like your 'good morning' better." Maybe this morning-after stuff wasn't too hard after all.

"So do I." He kissed her again and showed her how much he liked it by pulling her hips against his. By the time he broke this kiss, they were both breathing heavily and the bacon was in danger of burning. Brent grabbed the pan off the stove. "Another minute, and you would have to go hungry."

She handed him the empty plate sitting next to the stove as he started to pull the bacon from the pan. "Another minute, and I wouldn't have cared." She swiped a strip of bacon and took a bite.

He moaned. "Now you tell me." He took a bite from the piece of bacon she held out to him. A look of concern flashed in his eyes. Around his chewing he asked, "How are you feeling?"

She grinned and said, "Wonderful!" A shy, hesitant answer was totally beyond her, especially after the fantastic way he had said "good morning." If Brent didn't like her enthusiastic response, he never should have kissed her. After the night he had walked out on her and ended up in a barroom brawl, she'd promised herself she would never lie to him again, and that included holding back the truth. If they were going to have a relationship, it was going to be founded on trust. She trusted Brent enough to tell him the truth.

He placed the plate of bacon on the counter and lifted the frying pan full of eggs from the burner. Turning back to her, he pulled her into his arms. "Oh, Em."

She heard the catch in his voice and smiled against his shirt. The blue shirt smelled like lemons, fresh air, and just a hint of Brent's aftershave. His arms felt like heaven. She raised her head. "You're the only one who has ever called me that."

"What?" His thumb traced the curve of her jaw as he gazed hungrily at her mouth.

"You call me Em sometimes." She rubbed her cheek against his hand, as if she were a cat showing affection. Last night in his bed he had whispered the shortened version of her name, and he had shouted it in ecstasy. Both ways had caused her pleasure. No one had ever cared enough before to give her a nickname.

His fingertip stroked the delicate pink flesh of her lower lip. "Does it bother you?"

"No, I like it." She parted her lips and nipped at his finger. When he moaned with pleasure and the hungry look in his eyes changed to heated need, she sucked the finger into her mouth and wrapped her tongue around it. The shiver that shook his body was echoed in her own. She wanted Brent as much now as she had last night. How could he make her weak with need and moist with desire while cooking breakfast? To experience for the first time the desire between a man and a woman was remarkable. But to keep on experiencing it, time and time again, with Brent was both frightening and exhilarating. One minute she was afraid as to where it all would end, and the next terrified that it would end. A night with Brent had shown her one very important thing: She wanted more than to be just his partner on the farm. How much more she wasn't sure. She was still trying to deal with the fact that Brent had actually wanted her after learning about Jack. Brent made her feel special. He also made her feel like a woman. And contrary to what her father had taught her over the years, a woman did possess a certain power over a man that had nothing to do with cooking or cleaning. She had seen it in Brent's gaze last night, felt it in the way his body trembled when she touched him, and heard it in his voice. That certain little catch that spoke volumes gave him away every time. And she was seeing it now. Brent wanted her as much as she wanted him.

She released his finger and placed a teasing kiss at the corner of his mouth. She chuckled when he tried to turn his head to deepen the kiss. "Brent?"

"Hmmm . . ." He closed his eyes and smiled as she continued to string light kisses over his face.

"I think your beautiful breakfast is going to go to waste."

She stroked her tongue over his lips and heard him growl before swinging her up into his arms. "We can always reheat it later," he said as he carried her down the hall.

Much later they ended up throwing out the congealed eggs and reheating the bacon in the microwave. For the first time in the seven years Emma had been working at the farm, the chickens didn't receive their food and fresh water until after ten o'clock in the morning, and they didn't even seem to notice.

Brent glanced at the nest full of eggshells and baby chicks. Another nine beautiful chicks had made their arrival in the usual way. He knew he should be used to this by now, but he wasn't. Since his own arrival at the farm over a month earlier, he had witnessed hundreds of cracking eggs, tiny peeps, and wet, ugly birds drying out to be soft, fluffy yellow chicks. He never tired of the sight, though. Emma had commented more than once on his fascination with the baby chicks. That morning, while sitting on a wooden crate watching the last chick emerge, he had figured out what intrigued him so.

The chick reminded him of himself. The eggshell represented his life growing up. He had been totally surrounded and protected from the world by thick walls of expensive schools, proper housekeepers, servants, and money. His mother had even made the soft clucking sounds as the hen did to her brood. He knew his mother didn't have half the maternal instinct the hen possessed, but she managed to cluck so prettily whenever she wanted to impress her friends. Mrs. Butterfield, his mother's housekeeper, would have made a wonderful brooding hen.

He'd emerged from his shell the day he graduated from college and set out on his own. His mother had a job already lined up for him in the company that husband number four owned. He turned the job down and listened to an earful of his mother's clucking. That little fit was nothing compared to the one she treated him to the day he told her he'd just signed with a top modeling agency in New York. From her reaction, someone would think he had committed a crime instead of starting a career.

The years he was a model constituted his ugly-wet-bird phase. He knew he wasn't physically ugly, but he had felt awkward and unfulfilled in the fast-paced world of modeling. He never fit in with the hectic lifestyle, the endless rounds of parties, and the backstabbing politics that went on behind the scenes. At the end he only wanted one thing, and that was out. Financially he was secure, but mentally he was adrift. He didn't know what he would do when he left modeling. The answer was given to him by his grandfather's will.

Since the day he stepped foot on the Amazing Grace Farm he had felt a rightness. Physical labor, while hard and often tedious, was rewarding. He could see what he accomplished at the end of the day. The chickens depended on him. Emma depended on him. People who walked into grocery stores looking for something to cook for dinner depended on him. His feathers were drying out.

If physical work made his feathers dry out, Emma made them fluff. He wanted to pound on his chest, conquer the world, slay any dragons threatening her castle. He was in love, and never in his life had he been happier. There were still some bumpy patches that needed to be ironed out, like telling her he loved her, making Roddman pay for what he had done to Em, and maybe even explaining a tad more about his modeling career.

For the past week Emma had spent every night in his bed teaching him things he'd never known, like the sweetness of making love to the woman he loved. The rightness that shattered his soul when he reached his climax in the same instant as she. The comfort of holding her while she slept and the joy of waking every morning with her next to him. He wanted to spend the rest of his life waking up next to Emma.

Brent came out of his musing when a shaft of sunlight streaked across the nesting house floor and thirty-two hens started to cluck frantically. He glanced up and smiled at Emma standing in the doorway with the sun streaming in behind her. He would know her silhouette anywhere.

"Come on in before our mother hens have heart failure," he said.

Brooding hens were famous for their worrying. They didn't like strange noises, people, or sudden changes in their environment. The nesting house was lit by a couple of low-wattage lights, and the little amount of sunlight that filtered in through the screened-in vents cut high on the walls. There were also three small openings cut in the back wall that led to a fenced-in area, so the hens could get some fresh air, eat a few tasty bugs, exercise, and enjoy conjugal visits with one of the farms strutting roosters. Emma had named all nine roosters after popular male movie stars. Mel was currently holding court and preening with three hens in one corner of the fenced-in area. Kevin, Tom, and Harrison each had their own following. The rest of the local studs were taking the afternoon off by sleeping in the shadiest, coolest spot they could find, which happened to be in the corner of the nesting house. Three overhead fans were creating a nice breeze while keeping the air circulating.

Brent watched as Emma closed the door and walked toward him. Most of the hens' nervous clucking had died down. The hens all knew Emma. His heart constricted with happiness when she stopped directly in front of him, bent down, and kissed his cheek. She did it as naturally as if she had been doing it for years.

"I figured I'd find you in here." She shook her head and glanced around at the nesting boxes filled with hens, eggs, and some newly hatched chicks.

"We got another family to move over to the nursery tomorrow." He reached into the nearest nesting box and softly touched the heaving side of the wet chick still lying there. Eight fluffy siblings and the hen clucked and peeped. "How come chickens are so neurotic?"

"It's just their way." Emma made a tender calming noise to settle the family down.

"Do you think they know they'll become some-one's dinner?" He now understood Emma's insis-tence on never eating chicken. It had nothing to do with seeing, hearing, and smelling the animals all day, but more to do with not knowing if at one time you'd raised the animal you were currently sinking your teeth into. He didn't think he could ever eat chicken again either.

"It's been my experience that if you took the seven hundred chickens living on this farm and combined their brains, it still wouldn't equal a whole one." She reached up to pet the hen sitting in the box above the newly hatched family, and al-most received a fierce nip for her efforts.

Brent marveled at her quick reflexes. Emma knew instinctively when one of the chickens or hens was about to nip her. He hadn't developed that skill yet, as the red marks across his fingers could verify, but he was learning quickly. He had taken Emma's advice and never tried to touch one of the roosters. "I have to agree with you, Em." He chuckled as the hen in another box allowed Emma to stroke her head. "They aren't the most intelligent animals, are they?"

"No." She bent down and examined a family of eight that had hatched during the night. "But they are cute." She ignored the hen's loud clucking and picked up one of the chicks.

Brent reached over and gave the little fellow a gentle stroke with his finger. He had always known Emma cared about the chicks as much as he did, but she'd hidden it. In the past weeks, however, he'd seen her cuddle a baby chick, laugh at some of their silly antics, and softly croon to a fretful hen.

He'd also noticed other subtle changes in Emma. She was growing more feminine. Not that she wasn't one hundred percent woman before. Now she was just showing it more. At night, after the work was done and they'd cleaned up for dinner, she'd leave her hair loose and flowing down her back. She'd bought a couple of sleeveless blouses, in soft pastels or flowery prints, and started to wear them instead of men's baggy T-shirts. The night before, not only did she bake a cherry pie, but he actually smelled perfume behind her ears. The intoxicating fragrance had driven him to carry her upstairs and find out exactly where else she might have dabbed the flowery scent. She had been shocked and delighted at some of the spots he had examined.

Without devoting sixteen hours a day to the

farm, Emma was more relaxed and was having the time to discover who "Emma" was. There was a playful side to her that Brent never would have guessed at, until she helped him deliver feed and water to one of the runs that was nothing but a huge mud pit after all the rain they had had. Both of them had ended up rolling in the mud, looking for one of her boots that had been sucked off by the calf-high gunk. Her laughter had been the sweetest sound this side of heaven, and he had caused it. Every night her confidence in herself as a sexy, desirable woman grew. She explored more. Wanted more. Dared more.

Brent shifted his weight as rock-hard desire threatened to burst the zipper of his jeans. Even the memories of their lovemaking were enough to cause him discomfort. He instinctively knew her self-discovery was good, just as his was. But what if she discovered she didn't like being half partner in a chicken farm? What if she wanted to see the world? Join the Peace Corps? Star in a rock-and-roll band? Hell, if Brent Haywood, world-renowned model, could find contentment, peace, and love on a rundown chicken farm in some remote part of Arkansas, Emma Jane Carson, chicken farm expert, could become the next franchise queen of America. He knew it was a heck of a chance—all he wanted to do was carry Emma into the house, lock the door, and keep this precious jewel to himself— but he had to give her the space and time to grow.

He watched as she picked up another baby

chick and cradled it in her hands. The smile pulling at her mouth was telling. She was charmed by the little fellow, and the chick appeared to be warm and secure within her hands. Emma would make a wonderful mother. "Em?"

"Hmmm . . ." She started to put the baby chick back with his mother and siblings..

"Do you want children?" He cringed when Emma nearly dropped the chick. He hadn't meant to startle her. "I mean, do you ever think of settling down and raising kids instead of chickens?"

She took a long time settling the chick before straightening up and facing Brent. "Sure, I've thought about it."

"Why haven't you?" Now that he had gotten to know Emma, he couldn't imagine why someone hadn't married her years ago. He'd be eternally grateful that no one had, but it was still a mystery.

She shrugged and looked somewhere over his right shoulder. "Guess the right man never came along."

Brent nodded, as if her simple reply explained it all. It didn't. If he had to take a guess, he would say Emma had never gone looking for the right man. But who could blame her, with her experience with men? Her father was a drunk who'd chased away her mother when Emma was just a toddler. Her brothers, except for Jimmie's intervention the other night, followed in dear old Dad's footsteps. Jack Roddman was scum. And she had spent the last seven years of her life living and working with his grandfather, the grouch of Strawberry Ridge. It was a hell of a sorry lot to represent the male population, but it had to Emma. If he gave it some serious thought, he would be floored that she had dropped her guard long enough to let him in.

"If the right man ever comes along, will you want children?" He was praying he could be that right man. He could just picture Emma pregnant with his child. Of course, it would be hell trying to keep her off a tractor and out of the runs.

She busied herself with another hen, this one closer to the door. "Sure."

"How many?"

She moved even closer to the door and refused to look at him. "As many as I can afford." She opened the door. "I have to go check on something in the nursery. I'll meet you back at the house later."

Brent frowned as she hurried through the door and out into the sunlight. He hadn't meant to scare her away with his questions about children, but he wanted to know. He wanted kids. He needed to know that Emma hadn't been scared off by a mother who'd deserted her and a father who'd abused her. She hadn't. She wanted children. A farm full of brainless chickens, Emma, and children all figured into his plans for the future. Now all he needed to know was how Emma felt about the stupid chickens and him.

Emma looked across the table at her brother Jimmie and realized how much he had changed. The other week in the sheriff's office she had paid more attention to his swollen eye and busted mouth than to his appearance. Jimmie looked much older than his twenty-six years. His misspent youth had finally caught up to him. "I'm glad you could join me for lunch," she said.

He shrugged and continued to study the old laminated menu. "No problem."

She didn't know what to say or where to begin. The night before, she had been flabbergasted when she opened the phone book and saw that there was a separate listing for Jimmie Carson. She had been more shocked when she dialed the number and Jimmie answered. Her brother had been home on a Friday night, and by the lack of noise in the background, she would have to guess he was alone. "I'm not taking you from anything important, am I?"

"Nothing that can't wait." He glanced up at Rosie, the waitress. "The usual."

Emma smiled at Rosie. "Make that two." She handed the waitress the menus, and Rosie strolled back into the kitchen. Emma turned to Jimmie. "So, what have you been doing with yourself all these years?"

Over the years she had run into Jimmie in town and only stopped long enough for a quick hi and bye. Maybe it was time to stop blaming her brothers for her upbringing and lay that charge right where it belonged, at her father's and mother's doorstep. Her mother never should have left. If the marriage was that bad, she should have at least taken the kids with her when she split. To leave three boys under the age of seven and a two-and-a-half-year-old girl behind was cruel.

For his part, her father should have taken her mother's leaving as a warning and straightened his act out. Instead, he had only gotten worse. Her brothers were simply products of their environment, just as she was. While she was being treated like a slave, they had been praised for being male. The more trouble they had gotten into, the more her father had patted them on their backs and proudly proclaimed them as his sons. If they failed in school, it was okay. If they got drunk and stayed out all night, they were just being boys. If they treated their little sister as garbage, they were just following Dad's example.

Jimmie didn't look comfortable talking to his own sister, and that was sad. Emma had been hoping that with all the attention Dad had showered on him, Lenny, and Harlan, they would turn out all right. She knew it was an unrealistic hope, but she had had it anyway. Jimmie didn't look like he'd turned out any better than she had. At least she was now half owner of a seventy-acre chicken farm. It was the most a Carson had ever accomplished in this town in over a hundred years.

Jimmie toyed with his spoon for a long time. "I never should have let him treat you that way."

She knew instinctively who he was referring to.

Their father. "It wasn't your fault, Jimmie. I see that now."

"We should have stood up for you."

"If I'm not mistaken, you did that the other week in the Buds and Suds when you helped Brent."

"Yeah, well . . ." He pleated his napkin down the center. "You don't have to worry about Roddman any longer."

"Why?" She didn't like the burning feeling scorching the lining of her stomach. What had her brother done now?

"Lenny, Harlan, and me took care of that. We should have handled it years ago, but we didn't know." The napkin was pressed in half again. "You should have told us, but we know why you didn't."

She couldn't bring herself to tell him that they should have noticed she wasn't home that night and should have gone looking for her. Jimmie looked defeated enough. "It's past history." She smiled at Rosie as she placed two cups of coffee in front of them and left. "Do I want to know what you did to Jack?"

"Nothing illegal, if that's what you're afraid of." Jimmie smiled for the first time. "Let's just say he had to leave town in a hurry and isn't expected back for a long time."

Emma swallowed hard. "What about his uncle Frank?"

"What about him?"

"Isn't he upset?"

"Don't know. Don't care." Jimmie poured some cream into his coffee. "Let's drop that subject and move on to a better one. How's Haywood treating you?"

Emma felt herself turn red as she stammered, "F-fine." Her brother knew how to turn the cards around mighty quick. Here she invited him to lunch to learn more about him, and he was the one asking the questions.

"He seemed like an okay guy." Jimmie took a sip of coffee and watched her.

"He is." Emma couldn't believe that she'd just agreed to calling the man she was in love with "an okay guy." There was no hiding from the truth, and the truth was she loved Brent. Had been in love with him for weeks now. She wasn't sure exactly when it had happened, but it had. The other day when he'd started talking about children, it had hit her like a bolt of lightning. She was in love with him. She wanted Brent for more than just a bed partner. She wanted him forever. When he'd started to ask about children and how many she wanted, she had been afraid to reveal her love. What if she was reading something into his questions that wasn't there? Still, men didn't start talking about babies and such unless they were serious. Brent had never declared his love, but every day her hopes increased. He talked about the improvements they were going to make to the farm and the house. Every night, he carried her to heaven and showed her the power and the joy of being a woman. And for all of this, she referred to him as "an okay guy."

"Heard he settled up with the owner of the Buds and Suds and they dropped all charges," Jimmie said.

"Amazing how that happened, wasn't it?" She raised an eyebrow and waited.

Jimmie grinned. "Wasn't it."

"I don't want to know, do I?"

"Nope." He gave Rosie a flirtatious wink as she set two platters, overflowing with thick hamburgers and fries, down in front of them. "Consider it a gift, but make sure you thank Harlan the next time you run across him."

"Why the sudden change of heart?" Now she had two brothers to thank.

"When you left home, we were too young, stupid, and mostly drunk to realize you were our sister and needed protection. During the past seven years you never once showed any weakness, asked us for a favor, or seemed to need us for any reason. You ignored us, which hurt but we understood why. You seemed content to leave things as they were, and we allowed it because we owed it to you." He ran a hand through his hair and sighed. "When Roddman started shooting off his mouth, I realized we'd failed you more than we had known. If Brent hadn't shut Roddman up, I would have."

Emma blinked back the tears in her eyes. "Dammit, Jimmie. You say the sweetest things."

He looked horrified either at the thought of

saying sweet things or at her tears. "Don't you dare cry." He shoved a paper napkin across the table toward her. "You never cried at home."

She sniffled and blotted her eyes with the napkin. "People change in seven years."

Jimmie glanced at her light pink blouse with its flowery print on it and the way she wore her hair, all loose and flowing down her back. "There's a softness about you now, Emma. It wasn't there before." He gave her a knowing smile. "I'd say Haywood has a lot to do with your changes."

Emma smiled back. "I'd say you're right."

Emma pulled the dress off her closet door and held it up in front of her for the fifth time. It was gorgeous, red, and flowing. It was the perfect dress for the dinner and dancing Brent had promised her. They were going to drive down to Newport to some fancy restaurant. She had even heard Brent on the phone making reservations. She had never been to a restaurant where you had to make reservations. For that matter, she'd never been on a date with Brent, and they'd been lovers for two weeks already. She held the satiny bodice against her breasts and twirled around one more time. The full skirt whirled around her bare legs.

After leaving Jimmie at the diner that afternoon, she had headed for the only department store in town. She'd found the dress on a discount rack, and even at that price it had set her back a nice

chunk of cash. The matching red high heels had
cost more than the dress, but she hadn't been able
to resist. Add the price of pantyhose, red lace panties, and a red strapless bra, and she'd nearly blown a
month's wages. One more stop in the store had
proved her downfall. She'd purchased twenty
bucks' worth of makeup, along with three glamour
magazines for tips. She wanted Brent to be proud
to be seen with her. No boots, no jeans, and no
cursing tonight. Tonight she wanted to be his lady.

She finished toweling herself off and ran a comb
through her freshly washed hair. The first thing she
needed to do was glance through the magazines
and see what hints they had on applying the
makeup she'd bought. She would worry about telling Brent she didn't know how to dance later.

With an energetic bounce she threw herself
across the bed and grabbed the top magazine. The
model on the front cover looked plastic, starving,
and about eighteen years old. Great! Kids were going to show her how to dazzle Brent. She shook her
head and started turning pages. The picture dia-
gram on eyeshadows looked interesting but clown-
ish. Who ever heard of putting three different
shades of blue on one tiny eyelid? She glanced at
the fancy dresses models were wearing in the different ads and wondered what kept half of them up,
and what kept the other half from splitting at the
seam when you sat down.

She was halfway through the magazine when
she spotted him. Brent! She sat straight up on the

bed and squinted at the color ad. Her Brent was posing in an advertisement for Adonis cologne, if the small print at the bottom of the page was to be believed. In fact, Brent was Adonis. He was stretched out on a fluffy white cloud, totally naked with only a few strategic fluffs between him and immodesty. Three beautiful women, dressed in skimpy Greek-style gowns, surrounded him. One was feeding him grapes, one was pouring wine, and the third lay adoringly at his feet. Brent appeared to be enjoying all the attention.

Her teeth worried her lower lip as she studied the picture more closely. Brent wasn't wearing a stitch of clothing under that small fluff of cloud. He was stark naked, posing with three women, and enjoying himself. This was a long way from posing with men's flannel shirts, the latest sportswear, or even men's cotton briefs. Why would Brent tell her he modeled for catalogs, when he didn't? She glanced at the front cover again. It was a current issue of the magazine, so he obviously had posed for the ad recently.

She carefully tore a strip of paper off the next page and marked the spot. Then she looked through every page of all three magazines. Twenty minutes later she was fighting back tears. Brent was in a total of seven different advertisements. Four were for Adonis cologne, and each pose seemed more revealing and the women more beautiful. The other three were for various other products, and all contained exotic backgrounds and more sexy women in assorted states of undress.

Brent was the Adonis man! She wasn't so naive about life not to realize that Adonis cologne probably had at least a million-dollar ad campaign, and Brent was a very wealthy man. With the amount of money he made from modeling, he could probably buy the entire town, hell, maybe even the county. Brent Haywood was accustomed to the finer things in life. Magnificent apartments, fine food, and beautiful women. Emma glanced at her discount-rack dress hanging on the closet door and lost the battle against her tears.

She had only been fooling herself. Someone like Brent didn't fall in love with a backwoods chicken farmer when he had women like that falling at his feet. He obviously was only there for a short time, maybe for some well deserved R and R. He probably would never miss the money he was loaning the farm, or worse, he was using it for a tax write-off. That meant he was only using her for a convenient bed partner while he played at being a gentleman farmer.

She swiped at the tears rolling down her face as she stood up and slowly walked over to her dresser. In one motion she swept all the makeup she had just purchased into the dented wastebasket beside the dresser. The tears continued to flow as she flung the sexy red underwear across the room and tossed the shoes after it. The dress landed in a wrinkled heap in the corner of the room. All three magazines joined the makeup in the trash can.

Her father had used her. Jack had used her. Even Levi, in his own way, had used her. She would not allow Brent to use her. This was a new Emma. A stronger Emma. One who wouldn't allow anyone to use her ever again. Not even the man she loved.

Three minutes later she entered the living room to find Brent, dressed in a suit, loading a CD into his stereo. She straightened her shoulders, ignored how fabulous he looked in the handsome gray suit, and concentrated on making it through the next couple of minutes. In a voice thick with tears she said, "I want you gone by morning."

Brent spun around and stared at her. His gaze raked over her, noting her boots, jeans, and T-shirt in confusion. "You're not dressed?"

"I'm wearing more clothes than you do half the time."

"What are you talking about?"

She picked up her truck keys from the coffee table. She couldn't stay there another minute. She needed to put some space between them. "I don't care if you stop the loan to the farm or even trash whatever you fixed up in the house. If you want to sell, just tell me your price and I'll make arrangements with the bank to buy you out." She had no idea if she could even swing such a deal, but she would move heaven and earth trying. She walked out of the room.

"Emma, what's going on?" Brent asked as he followed her into the hallway.

"It's over." She opened the screen door. "Finished, kaput."

"Why?"

The pain in his voice brought a fresh wave of tears to her eyes. He honestly sounded upset, as if it mattered to him. "I thought we shared something special, Brent."

"We do." He took a step nearer.

"No, what we had was an illusion of love." She rubbed at a wayward tear and felt the trembling in her hands. "I thought we were building not only a better farm, but a future together."

"We were."

"Built on what? Lies?" She shook her head, stepped out onto the porch, and closed the screen door. "Where was the trust, Brent?" She'd promised herself no more lies, no more half-truths. Brent would probably be gone by morning, returning to city life and beautiful models. "I fell in love with you." There, she'd said it.

"Em . . ." He reached for the handle of the screen door.

"Good-bye, Brent." She wanted to scream. She wanted to curse. But all she did was walk down the steps, jump into old Betsy, and drive off.

ELEVEN

Brent picked up two buckets filled with feed and entered the run. Over a hundred chickens strutted, clucked, and generally got under his feet as he tried to fill the feed bins. Emma had been right. The creatures were so stupid they didn't even bother to get out of his way when he was trying to feed them. The confidence he had been feeling about Emma returning soon was beginning to fade. She had now been gone for three nights, and it was going on the fourth day. It felt as if she had been gone forever.

A surprise that he had ordered over a week ago had arrived two days earlier. She hadn't been home to see it. The money she had saved him by dickering with the salesman when he had purchased his new truck, had gone toward a secondhand pickup that was in pretty good shape. It had taken over a week to have a water tank installed into the bed, complete with a hose and enough pressure to clean out chicken coops. Never again would Emma have to haul buckets of water to the runs. Now it would be as simple as dragging a hose, and she hadn't been there to appreciate the beauty and ingenuity of his surprise. He'd also had them build a water-proof container that would hold about two hundred pounds of feed with a spout at the bottom, so Emma or he could fill buckets instead of hauling fifty-pound bags around. Fill it once and it should last for days.

He finished feeding and watering the last run, and it was barely nine o'clock in the morning. He had been up before dawn, a short three hours after he had hit the bed. He couldn't sleep. He couldn't eat. Fixing up the house held no appeal. Even cut-ting the grass felt like it was shredding his heart. This farm might be his heritage, but it wasn't a home without Emma.

After she had stormed out the other night and the shock had worn off, he'd gone upstairs to her room, the last place she had been. Whatever had set her off had to be in there, because twenty min-utes before that, she had waltzed out of the bath-room all squeaky-clean with only a towel wrapped around her. He had tried to corner her in the up-stairs hallway, but she had only flirted and prom-ised him the surprise of his life. She had surprised him all right.

His search through her room had nearly broken his heart. She had gone out and purchased a mind-blowing red dress and the works. He rehung the dress and folded the sexy scraps of lace she called underwear. He was still confused until he found the makeup and the magazines in the wastebasket. Emma had seen him between the glossy covers of glamour magazines. His omission of truth about what kind of a model he had been had come back to haunt him. More accurately, it had driven Emma away. When he glanced through the magazines, his heart sank further. The Adonis ads were in every one of them. When she had opened the pages, spread out before her had been full-page photos of him reclining in naked splendor, surrounded by fawning women. The shock of realizing this was the same man who worked right beside her cleaning out chicken coops must have been mind-boggling. No wonder she had run. No one in their right mind would believe the Adonis Man would be content living and working on a chicken farm and loving the sweetest woman on the face of the earth. But he was. He'd never liked the city lights when he was living in New York, and he surely wasn't missing them now. The only thing he was missing was Emma.

The night she left, he sat on the couch all night waiting for her to cool off and return. He ended up being awakened by the crowing of the roosters announcing dawn's arrival, not Emma's. At first he had been worried about where she went, but one thing he knew about Emma, she was resourceful, strong, and stubborn. She didn't seem to have any girlfriends or female companions she could go stay with. Her only family that he knew about were her father and brothers. He would wager every penny he'd made posing as the Adonis Man that Emma would rather sleep in a chicken coop than spend one night at her father's house. That eliminated her family, until he remembered Jimmie. After checking the phone book, he realized Jimmie wasn't living at home either. Emma might have gone to him. It was a big *might*, but it was the only place he could think of. The next morning he drove by, spotted old Betsy parked outside of Jimmie's mobile home, and knew where Emma had gone.

He didn't stop. Emma obviously was still upset, or she would have come home. So he drove back to the Amazing Grace Farm and a lonely old house. Yesterday he had packed up 131 chickens for the packers, then made sure the coop was cleaned out and ready for the next batch. That afternoon he was moving the 129 four-week-old chicks out of the nursery and into the cleaned run. It's what Emma would have done. Working the chicken end of the farm was a full-time job, and that wasn't counting the corn and hay fields. His respect and admiration for Emma had grown by leaps and bounds over the last few days. How she had managed to do it all was beyond him.

Brent parked the newly equipped truck in the barn and started to walk the fields. He didn't know the first thing about corn, hay, or actual farming. Emma had been handling that end of the work. She had taught him how to drive the tractor, but that wasn't doing him any good right now. He had no idea what to do with the chest-high corn or the hay that was reaching his knees. Everything about the place reminded him of Emma. His feet automatically took him to the huge maple tree at the top of the hill. He sat under the tree, as he had weeks before, and stared at the farm below.

Emma looked up from contemplating the bottom of her coffee cup and studied Jimmie as he puttered around the kitchen. It still shocked her every time she saw Jimmie actually do something in the kitchen, besides empty the refrigerator or leave empty beer bottles on the counter. Three nights ago, when she had showed up unannounced on his doorstep, she had been greeted with open arms and the promise she could stay as long as she liked. She liked the time she had spent with Jimmie, getting to know the man he'd become. She liked his neat if somewhat crowded mobile home. But she didn't like staying there. She missed the farm. She missed Brent.

Jimmie had surprised her. Not only had he passed his G.E.D. test and received his high school diploma, he had attended college at night while working a construction job up in Walnut Ridge. His teaching degree was framed and hanging next to his high school diploma in what should have been a spare bedroom. Jimmie had converted it into an office crammed with more books than a library. Sometime in late summer he would be moving up into the mountain regions of the Ozarks to start his teaching career. She had been wrong. Jimmie had accomplished more than owning half a chicken farm. He was the first Carson to receive a college degree.

"Do you want your eggs scrambled or fried?" he asked. He held up a couple of eggs and smiled.

"How about if I cook this morning? You go get ready for work." She got off the stool and walked around the counter to pick up the frying pan.

"What are you going to do all day? Sit around and mope?"

"I don't mope!" She snatched an egg from his hand.

Jimmie poured himself another cup of coffee. "Could have fooled me." He watched as she cracked all five eggs into a bowl and started to beat them. "Aren't you afraid Haywood's killing off half your birds?" When he got no response besides a very unladylike snort, he said, "I wouldn't want no city boy taking care of my livelihood."

"He knows how to care for them." She dumped the eggs into the heated pan. "I took care of his half for months, it's his turn now." Having Brent handling the chickens was the least of her worries. She had given him three days and nights to leave and head on back to the bright lights and the gorgeous women. The man didn't seem to be leaving. Every day after Jimmie had left for work, she had moped around until she couldn't stand it any longer. Then she had gone over to Tom Wentzel's place, climbed the ridge that bordered her property, and stood in the shadow of the huge oaks and spied on Brent. He had been handling the chickens as if he were born to it.

"Aren't you even going to try to talk to him?" Jimmie asked.

"Tired of me already?" She ran the spatula around the pan so that the eggs didn't stick and dry out. Jimmie hated dry eggs. She frowned at the pan. Old habits died hard.

"The offer to stay as long as you like is still open, Emma." He got down two plates and put a couple of pieces of bread in the toaster. "Haywood seemed like an okay guy to me." He stopped in the middle of taking the butter from the refrigerator as a suspicious thought hit him. "He didn't beat you or anything?"

"Of course not!" Emma exclaimed. How could anyone think such an offensive thing about Brent? The man was more mild-mannered than Clark Kent.

"So what the hell happened?"

"You want it in a nutshell?" Emma snapped. She was tired of Jimmie's questions and his quiet sympathetic looks. "Do you know what Brent did before he came here?" She scraped the frying pan with vicious strokes. "He was a model!"

Jimmie blinked twice. "A model?"

"Yes," Emma snarled. "A *fashion* model."

One corner of Jimmie's mouth twisted and

tilted upward. He tried to smother his laughter behind his hand and failed.

Emma waved the spatula at her brother. "Don't you dare laugh, James Stonewall Carson!" Tears pooled in her eyes. "It's not funny."

Jimmie's laughter immediately died at the look of distress on his sister's face. "I could think of worse things to be, sis. Parading around in your BVDs is an honest profession." He raised his eyebrow as if he had to think about that one for a moment.

"Most of the time he didn't even have them on," Emma cried.

"You mean he was naked!" It was Jimmie's turn to shout.

"No." A tear slipped down her cheek, and she angrily swiped it away with her fist. "He was covered by a cloud."

"A cloud!"

"Forget the cloud, Jimmie." She brushed that aside as if it were unimportant. "He was being drooled over by beautiful women wearing next to nothing!" There, she'd finally admitted what was really bothering her. It wasn't the fact that he had neglected to tell her exactly what kind of modeling he did. It was the women and what they represented. They symbolized the lifestyle Brent was used to. A lifestyle she didn't comprehend and could never hope to compete with.

Under his breath Jimmie said, "We should all

have it so hard." He took the eggs off the burner and shook his head. "He gave all that up to become a chicken farmer?"

"He didn't give it up." She walked around the counter and sat back down on a stool.

"He said he was going back?"

"No."

"Is he thinking of going back?" Jimmie scraped the eggs onto two plates and pushed one plate across the counter at her.

"He says no."

Jimmie handed her a fork and the salt and pepper shakers. "Sounds like he gave it up to me." He reached for the toast and started to butter it.

"What man in his right mind would give all that up?"

"A man who obviously found what he was looking for here." He handed her a slice of toast. "Why don't you eat your breakfast and go see how your chickens are doing?"

Emma pushed a hunk of egg to the other side of her plate. "You should have seen the women, Jimmie. They were beautiful."

He gave a slow, knowing smile. "When was the last time you looked in a mirror, Emma? Really looked?"

She shook her head as a tear fell onto her plate. "You're my brother."

"I'm a man, Emma." He placed a finger under her chin and raised her face. "I saw how he looked

at you that night at the jail. Not only does he think
you're beautiful, I'll bet my teaching degree that
the man's in love with you."

"Really?"

"Go home and find out."

A couple of hours later Emma drove old Betsy
up the graveled drive and stopped in front of the
house. She was taking the first piece of advice her
brother had ever offered: She was coming home to
find out if Brent loved her.

She stared out the cracked windshield at her
home. Sometime after Brent's arrival the house had
become a home to her. The porch was still sagging
and the paint faded, but the colorful flowers Brent
had planted a month ago were blooming. It offered
her a smidgen of hope that maybe something else
could bloom here, like love.

She climbed out of the truck and glanced
around the yard. It looked the same. Brent's new
pickup was parked by the barn. The nursery looked
to be overrun with nervous hens and curious chicks.
The chickens in run number three were happily out
of their enclosure looking for grubs and worms between dust bathing in the dry dirt. She noticed that
run number one stood empty. The packers must
have come yesterday, and today the four-week-old
chicks had to be moved from the nursery into the
run. Brent had managed very well without her.

Her gaze shot to the flash of red under the huge

maple tree on top of the hill. The one Brent had kissed her under. The one she considered *their* tree. She squinted against the sun and spotted Brent sitting on the grass looking down. He had sat there when he was pensive about his grandparents. Now he was sitting there again, and she couldn't help but wonder if he was thinking of her or of heading back to the bright lights. Emma took a deep breath, squared her shoulders, and headed for the hill.

Within minutes she sat down beside him and looked at the view. It hadn't changed much since the last time she'd looked at it. The corn was higher and the hay appeared to be ready for cutting in about another week. Same fields, same house, but a different Emma. For two hours after Jimmie had left for work that morning, she'd sat in the kitchen and thought. What if Jimmie was right? What if Brent was in love with her? Could she really throw it all away because of her own insecurities? Did she have the guts to face Brent and see where they stood? It had all seemed pretty hopeless to her, until she'd remembered one very important thing. Brent hadn't left yet, nor did it appear he was going to. Could he really be happy living on his grandparents' farm? She'd never know the answers to the questions screaming in her head until she asked.

She pulled her knees up and rested her chin on top of them. Shyly she glanced beneath her lashes at the man sitting beside her. Brent looked relaxed with his legs stretched out before him, resting back on his elbows, a blade of grass stuck between his lips. "You didn't leave yet."

"Nope." He continued to stare off into the distance.

"Are you going to?"

The grass was shifted to the other side of his mouth. "Nope."

"Are you happy here?"

"Yup."

"Are you turning into a hayseed?" She didn't like his one-syllable answers.

He raised an eyebrow and pulled the grass out of his mouth. His gaze raked her face as if he were starving for the sight of her. "I guess I have some explaining to do about my former career."

"You were a model, a very famous one from what I can gather."

"Not that famous." He gave a small chuckle, directed more at himself than the situation. "Not one person has recognized me since I've been here."

"If those ads had been placed in *Hunters-R-Us* or *Beer Drinking Buddies*, we would have had people lined up in the driveway begging for autographs."

This time his chuckle sounded sincere. "I'm afraid you might be right on that one, Emma. But you're wrong on some other stuff. I owe you an apology."

"For what? Not telling me you posed in front

of a high-priced camera instead of modeling camouflage for *Gut 'Em* magazine?"

"I should have been more explicit."

"If you had told me you went around posing in nothing more than a cloud, I probably would have locked you out of the house and called the sheriff."

Brent sat up straighter. "If you're not upset about my *ex*-modeling, what kept you at Jimmie's for four days?"

"You knew I was at Jimmie's?"

"You don't think I would have just let you walk out of the house without knowing where you were, did you?" At her dazed look, he groaned. "Oh, Em. I knew where you were since nine o'clock the next morning. I kept away so you would have the time and space you needed to figure out how mad you were at me."

"I wasn't mad, Brent." She looked away from his silver eyes, which seemed to be promising her the world if she gave him a chance. "I was hurt and confused, but mostly I was scared."

"Scared of what?"

"Never being enough." Those three simple words managed to say it all. She would never be beautiful enough, rich enough, smart enough, elegant enough, sexy enough, proper enough, or woman enough to hold Brent. All her life she had never been enough.

"Enough what?"

"Enough anything, Brent." She turned her

head and held his gaze. "When I saw all those beautiful women posing with you, I realized how I must appear to you with my work boots, baggy shirts, and Southern accent."

"Your accent is adorable. Your work boots aren't any dirtier than mine. And I love what's under your baggy shirts." He moved closer and cupped her cheek. "Haven't you realized that yet?"

"What about your old life? Don't you miss the good things in life? Like fancy cooking, someone to do your cleaning, parties, and women hanging all over you?"

His thumb stroked the rapidly pounding pulse in her throat. "Emma, you are the good thing in my life. The very best thing that has ever happened to me." He tilted her chin up and kissed her lips. "I should have told you weeks ago, but I was saving it for a special occasion." He brushed her lips one more time. "I love you."

"How?"

"How?" He chuckled. "Beats me, Em. It was the easiest thing I've ever done."

"I don't mean that how, I mean how could you love someone like me?" She glanced down at herself and grimaced. She was wearing the same jeans and T-shirt she'd had on when she'd left the house. For the past few days she had been hand washing her undies and wearing Jimmie's sweats and shirts. "I'm not like the other women in your life."

"Thank God for small favors." Brent pulled her into his embrace. "Em, hasn't it occurred to you that if I wanted the city lights, the rat race, the fancy parties, and the glamour girls, I never would have left New York?"

"What about a college education and fancy degrees?"

"I haven't noticed that you're stupid, Em." He twirled a lock of her hair around a finger. "In fact, during the past couple of days my respect and admiration for you has grown immensely. I never realized everything involved with running this farm until you left. You deserve a medal for keeping it going on your own."

"It was called desperation, Brent." She had done a good job running the farm and keeping it out of the bankers' greedy hands. It hadn't required a fancy degree, just know-how and hard physical work. Maybe showy diplomas didn't count for as much as she'd thought. She couldn't imagine any of those long-nailed city women running the farm. "Even you can't deny the difference in our looks, though. The women in those ads were incredible."

"What does that have to do with us? I never dated any of those models." He frowned at her look of disbelief. "I won't deny that I never dated any models. Of course I did. Many of them, in fact. But those were the women I saw every day. I worked with them, partied with them, and had absolutely nothing in common with them. Don't you see, they're like hothouse lilies. Beautiful to look at, but take them out into the real world and they wilt

and die. You're like a garden rose. Beautiful, delicate, and strong. You can survive a winter's storm
and still come up each spring." His fingers stroked
the faint blush sweeping across her cheek.

"What about my mouth?"

He grinned. "Heaven to kiss, perfect in fit,
sweet to taste . . ."

"No, I meant my very unladylike tendency to
curse."

"I can live with it." He laughed. "Do you know
I have one hundred and fifty-two I.O.U.'s in the
jar?"

"You counted them?"

"Every night since you've been gone. I count
them, and then I sit there and fantasize how I'm
going to collect each and every one of them."

"Oh, my . . ." She was stunned, delighted, and
terribly excited. Brent had counted every one of
those slips of papers.

"One thing though," he said.

"What?"

He threaded his fingers through her hair and
held the back of her neck. "You're going have to
watch how many I.O.U.'s you create after the kids
start to come. We don't want to be teaching the
little ones bad habits."

"What kids?"

"The kids we're going to have just as soon as I
can talk Mrs. Butterfield into leaving my mother's
employment, hire contractors to add on a family

room and a couple more bathrooms, and convince you to marry me."

"You honestly think I'll need convincing?" Happiness bubbled inside her like champagne. She'd never tasted the fine beverage, but she'd once heard someone comment on how the bubbles tickled your nose when you drank it. She had thought it was silly at the time, but now she would swear bubbles were tickling every pore in her body.

"I'm willing to convince you," Brent muttered against her mouth.

"I'm willing to let you try." She melted into his kiss.

He deepened the kiss and pulled her down onto the soft, sweet-smelling grass. "Lord, how I missed you, Em."

"I missed you too." She recaptured his mouth and poured all her love into that one kiss. When she broke the kiss, she whispered, "That was one."

"One what?" he asked as he gasped for breath.

"You said there were a hundred and fifty-two." She nipped at his lower lip. "I'm going to make sure you get every one of those kisses." He wanted to marry her! Her brother's advice had been right. She owed Jimmie a lot, but first she had to repay Brent.

"Oh, Em. I do love you."

"I love you too. And I'll marry you on one condition."

His mouth was nuzzling the sensitive skin behind her ear as his fingers slid under her shirt. He raised his head and gazed down at her. "What?"

"The next time you have this hidden desire to dress your baby-maker in a cloud, I'd better be the only one there."

Brent threw back his head and laughed.

EPILOGUE

Emma stood on the freshly painted white porch with its wicker furniture and hanging Boston ferns and glared up at her husband and the keys he was holding over his head. "Hand them over, Haywood."

"I will not, Haywood." He kept them out of her reach. "The doctor said no more plowing after your fifth month." He glanced down at her rounded tummy and grinned. She looked way past her fifth month to him, and he should know. Emma was carrying their third child.

"You promised I could help." She placed her hands in the general area where her hips should have been. The flowery maternity top stretched across her abdomen, making her look bigger.

"You can help, Em." He quickly pocketed the keys.

"Doing what? Benjamin James is taking his nap,

and Sarah's in the kitchen helping Mrs. Butterfield bake cookies. The house is spotless, the laundry is done, and I haven't seen you since you left our bed at dawn."

Brent pulled her into his arms and kissed her. After all these years Emma still wasn't used to sitting around and relaxing. She constantly needed something to do. She wasn't like other women, who picked up hobbies, like knitting or sewing. No, Emma liked working the farm and was very active in every stage of it. Considering her condition, it was proving to be quite a challenge keeping her occupied. Em and Mrs. Butterfield handled the house, four-year-old Sarah, and two-year-old Ben. Never had two children been so loved.

He'd had to leave early that morning to spend some time over on the next farm. The Amazing Emma Farm was 212 acres of prime chicken ranch. It was the old Harris place that had bordered their farm to the east. He'd bought Harris out after the drought three years back. He had hired Emma's brother Lenny to manage it, so he could stay closer to home, the children, and Emma. "I have something in the barn that needs your opinion," he said.

Emma immediately brightened. "What?" She allowed Brent to grab her hand and lead her into what used to be the old barn. With fresh paint, major repairs, and lots of TLC, the barn looked and smelled new. Fresh hay was stored in half of it, and the new tractor along with the old John Deere were parked in the other half.

"It's over here." Brent hid his grin as he led Emma into the back part of the barn. An hour earlier he had set out a blanket over a pile of hay, an ice bucket with a bottle of grape juice in it, and two crystal glasses. He pulled her into what normally was a tack room.

Emma glanced at the scene and grinned. "You know me pretty well, don't you?"

"I know you well enough to know you'd be heading for the tractor and the upper hay field as soon as Benny went in for his nap."

"And you think this will keep my mind off the field or the fact that I can't drive a tractor for another five or six months?"

He helped her to sit down before sitting next to her and reaching into a small picnic basket. "I know the grape juice won't, but I am hoping this will." He held up a handful of white fluff that resembled a cloud, and grinned.

EINSTEIN AND PINK
ARE HAVING A BABY!
IS IT A BOY OR A GIRL?
HOW WILL THE PROUD PARENTS CHOOSE
A NAME?
PLEASE, THEY NEED YOUR HELP!

- You first met Einstein, everybody's favorite artificial intelligence computer, in Ruth Owen's debut novel MELTDOWN, LOVESWEPT #558.

- In SMOOTH OPERATOR, LOVESWEPT #632, Einstein met his match in PINK—a computer who could really blow his fuse!

- But their true love was tested in SORCERER, LOVESWEPT #714, when PINK had to save Einstein from a microchip/intelligence/byte threatening virus.

- Now Einstein and PINK are expecting a baby. The only problem is, they need a name. . . .

Read the Official Rules to find out what you need to do to enter LOVESWEPT'S NAME THE BABY COMPUTER CONTEST.

Now, share in PINK and Einstein's excitement as they await their new arrival, and win a chance to give them the gift that will last a lifetime!

LOVESWEPT'S "NAME THE BABY COMPUTER" CONTEST
OFFICIAL RULES:

1. *No purchase is necessary.* Enter by printing or typing your name, address, and telephone number at the top of a piece of 8 ½" x 11" plain white paper, if typed, or lined paper, if handwritten. Below your name and address, write the name (and gender) you're suggesting for Einstein's and PINK's baby, and an essay of no more than 100 words explaining what gave you the idea for the suggested name for the baby computer. If you need inspiration, Einstein was first introduced to LOVESWEPT readers in MELTDOWN by Ruth Owen, Einstein met PINK in Ruth Owen's SMOOTH OPERATOR, and their true love was tested in Ruth Owen's SORCERER. Each of these books is readily available in libraries. Once you've completed your entry form, mail your entry to: LOVESWEPT'S "NAME THE BABY COMPUTER" CONTEST, Dept. SS, Bantam Books, 1540 Broadway, New York, NY 10036.

2. PRIZES (3): *First Prize (1)*: The name suggested by the First Prize winner will be the name used for Einstein's and PINK's baby in Ruth Owen's next LOVESWEPT novel (scheduled for publication in May 1996). The First Prize winner also will be profiled and pictured in the back of that book as well as in the back of the other May 1996 LOVESWEPTs and will receive autographed copies of each of Ruth Owen's LOVESWEPT novels involving Einstein and PINK. (Approximate retail value: $15.00.) *Second Prize (2)*: The two Second Prize winners will receive autographed copies of the May 1996 Ruth Owen LOVESWEPT novel which introduces the baby computer and also will be named in the back of that book and the other May 1996 LOVESWEPTs as runners up to the First Prize winner. (Approximate retail value: $4.50.)

3. Contest entries must be postmarked and received by August 1, 1995, and all entrants must be 21 or older on the date of entry. The entries submitted will be judged by Ruth Owen and members of the LOVESWEPT Editorial Staff on the basis of the originality and creativity shown in the choice of a name for the baby computer and the thoughtfulness and writing ability reflected in the accompanying essay. If there are insufficient entries or if, in the judge's sole opinion, no entry contains a suitable name for the baby computer, Bantam reserves the right not to declare a winner for either or both Prizes. If Bantam determines not to award the First Prize, any winners selected for the Second Prize will receive an autographed copy of the May 1996 Ruth Owen LOVESWEPT which introduces the baby computer but will not be named in the back of that book and the other May 1996 LOVESWEPTs. All of the judges' decisions are final and binding. All essays must be original. Entries become the property of Bantam Books and will not be returned. Bantam Books is not responsible for incomplete or lost or misdirected entries.

4. Winners will be notified by mail on or about September 1, 1995. Winners have 14 days from the date of notice in which to accept their prize award or an alternate winner will be chosen. Odds of winning are dependent on the number of entries received. Prizes are non-transferable and no substitutions are allowed. Winners may be required to execute an Affidavit Of Eligibility And Promotional Release supplied by Bantam Books and the First Prize Winner will need to supply a photograph for inclusion in the one-page profile. Entering the Contest constitutes permission for use of the winner's name, address (city and state), photograph, biographical profile, and the name and essay submitted for publicity and promotional purposes, with no additional compensation.

5. Employees of Bantam Books, Bantam Doubleday Dell Publishing Group, Inc., their subsidiaries and affiliates, and their immediate family members are not eligible to enter. This Contest is open to residents of the U.S. and Canada, excluding the Province of Quebec, and is void wherever prohibited or restricted by law. Taxes, if any, are the winner's sole responsibility.

6. The winners of the Contest will be announced in Ruth Owen's May 1996 LOVESWEPT novel as well as in other LOVESWEPTs published in May 1996.

THE EDITORS' CORNER

Be sure to scope out a spot in the shade to share with the four sultry LOVESWEPT romances headed your way next month. This picnic packs a menu of intoxicating love stories spiced with passion and a hint of fate.

USA Today bestselling author Patricia Potter cooks up an intoxicating blend of conflict and emotions in her latest, **IMPETUOUS**, LOVESWEPT #746. Like an exotic gypsy, PR whiz Gillian Collins sweeps into Steven Morrow's office and begins her crusade to win his consent for a splashier grand opening of his latest project! He's always preferred practical, reliable, safe—but Gillian enchants him, makes him hunger for pleasures he's never known. Patricia Potter demonstrates how good it can be when the course of true love doesn't quite run smooth.

Judy Gill offers double doses of love and laughter with **TWICE THE TROUBLE,** LOVESWEPT #747. Maggie Adair is magnificent when riled, John Martin decides with admiration—no lioness could have protected her cub more fiercely! But once Maggie learns that her adopted daughter and his were twins separated at birth, shock turns to longing for this man who can make them a family, a lover who needs her fire. Judy Gill transforms a surprising act of fate into this witty, touching, and tenderly sensual romance.

The moment she sees the desert renegade, Carol Lawson instantly knows Cody Briggs is her **DREAM LOVER,** LOVESWEPT #748, by Adrienne Staff. Seeing the spectacular mesa country through his eyes awakens her senses, makes her yearn to taste forbidden fire on his lips—but when Cody offers to trade his secrets for hers, she runs. Mesmerizing in emotion, searing in sensuality, this spellbinding tale of yearning and heartbreak, ecstasy and betrayal, is Adrienne Staff's most unforgettable novel yet.

With more sizzle than a desert at high noon, Gayle Kasper presents **HERE COMES THE BRIDE,** LOVESWEPT #748. Nick Killian's underwear is as wicked as his grin, Fiona Ames thinks as the silk boxers spill all over the luggage carousel from his open suitcase! She's flown to Las Vegas to talk her father out of marrying Nick's aunt, never expecting to find an ally in the brash divorce lawyer. When the late-night strategy sessions inspire a whirlwind romance, Nick vows it won't last. Can Fiona show him their love is no mirage? Experience Gayle Kasper's special talent for creating delectable characters whose headlong fall into love is guaranteed to astonish and delight.

Happy reading!

With warmest wishes,

Beth de Guzman

Shauna Summers

Beth de Guzman
Senior Editor

Shauna Summers
Associate Editor

P.S. Watch for these spectacular Bantam women's fiction titles slated for July: From *The New York Times* bestselling author Amanda Quick comes her newest hardcover, **MYSTIQUE**, a tantalizing tale of a legendary knight, a headstrong lady, and a daring quest for a mysterious crystal; fast-rising star Jane Feather spins a dazzling tale of espionage in **VIOLET** in which a beautiful bandit accepts a mission more dangerous than she knows; **MOTHER LOVE**, highly acclaimed Judith Henry Wall's provocative new novel, tests the limits of maternal bonds to uncover what happens when a child commits an act that goes against a mother's deepest beliefs; in Pamela Morsi's delightful **HEAVEN SENT**, the preacher's daughter sets out to trap herself a husband and ends up with the local moonshiner and a taste of passion more intoxicating than his corn liquor; Elizabeth Elliott's spectacular debut, **THE WARLORD,** is a magical and captivating tale of a woman who must dare to love the man she fears the most. Check out next month's LOVESWEPTS for a sneak peek at these compelling novels. And immediately following this page, look for a preview of the wonderful romances from Bantam that *are available now!*

FAIREST OF THEM ALL

by best-selling author
TERESA MEDEIROS

*Teresa Medeiros has skyrocketed into the front ranks of
best-selling romance authors following the phenomenal success of THIEF OF HEARTS, WHISPER OF ROSES,
and ONCE AN ANGEL. FAIREST OF THEM ALL is
her most enchanting romance ever.*

*She was rumored to be the fairest woman in all of England. But Holly de Chastel considered her beauty a curse.
She had turned away scores of suitors with various ruses,
both fair and foul. Now she was to be the prize in a tournament of eager knights. Holly had no intention of wedding any of them and concocted a plan to disguise her
beauty. Yet she didn't plan on Sir Austyn of Gavenmore.
The darkly handsome Welshman was looking for a plain
bride and Holly seemed to fit the bill. When he learned
that he'd been tricked, it was too late. Sir Austyn was
already in love—and under the dark curse of Gavenmore.*

Sweeter than the winds of heav'n is my lady's
      breath,
Her voice the melodious cooing of a dove.
Her teeth are snowy steeds,
Her lips sugared rose petals,
That coax from my heart promises of love.

Holly smothered a yawn into her hand as the minstrel strummed his lute and drew breath for another
verse. She feared she'd nod off into her wine before
he got around to praising any attributes below her
neck. Which might be just as well.

A soulful chord vibrated in the air.

The envy of every swan is my lady's graceful
      throat,
Her ears the plush velvet of a rabbit's
Her raven curls a mink's delight.
But far more comely in my sight—

Holly cast the generous swell of her samite-clad
bosom a nervous glance, wondering desperately if
teats rhymed with *rabbit's*.

The minstrel cocked his head and sang, "are the
plump, tempting pillows of her—"

"Holly Felicia Bernadette de Chastel!"

Holly winced as the minstrel's nimble fingers tangled in the lutestrings with a discordant twang. Even
from a distance, her papa's bellow rattled the ewer of
spiced wine on the wooden table. Elspeth, her nurse,
shot her a panicked look before ducking so deep into
the window embrasure that her nose nearly touched
the tapestry she was stitching.

Furious footsteps stampeded up the winding stairs
toward the solar. Holly lifted her goblet in a half-

hearted toast to the paling bard. She'd never grown immune to her father's displeasure. She'd simply learned to hide its effects. As he stormed in, she consoled herself with the knowledge that he was utterly oblivious to the presence of the man reclining on the high-backed bench opposite her.

Bernard de Chastel's ruddy complexion betrayed the Saxon heritage he would have loved to deny. Holly's trepidation grew as she recognized the ducal seal on the wafer of wax being methodically kneaded by his beefy fist.

He waved the damning sheaf of lambskin at her. "Have you any idea what this is, girl?"

She popped a sweetmeat in her mouth and shook her head, blinking innocently. Brother Nathanael, her acerbic tutor, had taught her well. A lady should never speak with her mouth occupied by other than her tongue.

Flicking away the mangled seal with his thumb, her papa snapped open the letter and read, " 'It is with great regret and a laden heart that I must withdraw my suit for your daughter's hand. Although I find her charms unparalleled in my experience' "—he paused for a skeptical snort—" 'I cannot risk exposing my heir to the grave condition Lady Holly described in such vivid and disturbing detail during my last visit to Tewksbury.' " Her father glowered at her. "And just what condition might that be?"

"Webbed feet," she blurted out.

"Webbed feet?" he echoed, as if he couldn't possibly have heard her correctly.

She offered him a pained grin. "I told him the firstborn son of every de Chastel woman was born with webbed feet."

Elspeth gasped in horror. The minstrel frowned

thoughtfully. Holly could imagine him combing his brain for words to rhyme with *duck*. Her father wadded up the missive, flushing scarlet to the roots of his graying hair.

"Now, Papa, are you *that* eager to see me wed?"

"Aye, child, I am. Most girls your age are long wedded and bedded, with two or three babes at the hearth and another on the way. What are you waiting for, Holly? I've given you over a year to choose your mate. Yet you mock my patience just as you mock the blessing of beauty our good Lord gave you."

She rose from the bench, gathering the skirts of her brocaded cotehardie to sweep across the stone floor. "Blessing! 'Tis not a blessing, but a curse!" Contempt thickened her voice. " 'Holly, don't venture out in the sun. You'll taint your complexion.' 'Holly, don't forget your gloves lest you crack a fingernail.' 'Holly, don't laugh too loud. You'll strain your throat.' The men flock to Tewksbury to fawn and scrape over the musical timbre of my voice, yet no one listens to a word I'm saying. They praise the hue of my eyes, but never look *into* them. They see only my alabaster complexion!" She gave a strand of her hair an angry tug only to have it spring back into a flawless curl. "My raven tresses!" Framing her breasts in her hands, she hefted their generous weight. "My plump, tempting—" Remembering too late who she was addressing, she knotted her hands over her gold-linked girdle and inclined her head, blushing furiously.

The duke bowed his head, battling the pained bewilderment that still blamed Felicia for dying and leaving the precocious toddler to his care. Holly had passed directly from enchanting child with dimpled knees and tumbled curls to the willowy grace of a woman grown, suffering none of the gawkiness that so frequently plagued girls in their middle years.

Now she was rumored to be the fairest lady in all of England, all of Normandy, perhaps in all the world.

"I've arranged for a tournament," he said without preamble.

"A tournament?" she said lightly. "And what shall be the prize this time? A kerchief perfumed with my favorite scent? The chance to drink mulled wine from the toe of my shoe? A nightingale's song from my swan-like throat?"

"You. You're to be the prize."

Holly felt the roses in her cheeks wither and die. She gazed down into her father's careworn face, finding its gravity more distressing than anger. She towered over him by several inches, but the mantle of majesty he had worn to shield him from life's arrows since the death of his beloved wife added more than inches to his stature.

"But, Papa, I—"

"Silence!" He seemed to have lost all tolerance for her pleas. "I promised your mother on her deathbed that you would marry and marry you shall. Within the fortnight. If you've a quarrel with my judgment, you may retreat to a nunnery where they will teach you gratitude for the blessings God has bestowed upon you."

His bobbing gait was less sprightly than usual as he left Holly to contemplate the sentence he'd pronounced.

Dire heaviness weighted Holly's heart. *A nunnery.* Forbidding stone walls more unscalable than those that imprisoned her now. Not a retreat, but a dungeon where all of her unspoken dreams of rolling meadows and azure skies would rot to dust.

What are you waiting for, Holly? her papa had asked.

Her gaze was drawn west toward the impenetrable tangle of forest and craggy dark peaks of the Welsh mountains. A fragrant breath of spring swept through her, sharpening her nameless yearning. Genuine tears pricked her eyelids.

"Oh, Elspeth. What *am* I waiting for?"

As Elspeth stroked the crown of her head, Holly longed to sniffle and wail. But she could only cry as she'd been taught, each tear trickling like a flawless diamond down the burnished pearl of her cheek.

TEMPTING
MORALITY
by Geralyn Dawson

**"One of the best new authors to come along in
years—fresh, charming, and romantic!"***

*She was a fraud. That's what Zach Burkett thought when
he caught sight of Miss Morality Brown testifying at a
town meeting. A deliciously enticing fraud would be the
perfect cover for his scheme to pay back the "godly" folk of
Cottonwood Creek for their cruel betrayal. But Zach was
wrong: far from being a con, the nearly irresistible angel
was a genuine innocent. And only after he'd shamelessly
tempted her to passion would he discover that he'd endan-
gered his own vengeful heart.*

*He was the answer to her prayers. That's what Morality
Brown thought when she gazed up into Zach Burkett's
wicked blue eyes. It hardly mattered that the slow-
drawling, smooth-talking rogue was a self-confessed sinner,
or that she sensed a hidden purpose behind his charm. In
his arms, she found the heaven she'd always longed for. But
all too soon, she'd discover the terrible truth about the man
who'd stolen her heart. Scarred by the past, he lives for
revenge—and it will take a miracle of love to save his soul.*

* *New York Times* best-selling author Jill Barnett

Flickering torches cast shadows across the faces of the faithful gathered to hear Reverend J. P. Harrison, founder of the Church of the Word's Healing Faith, preach his message. Anticipation gripped the listeners as the reverend stepped up to the lectern, and the low-pitched murmur of voices died as he sounded out a greeting.

"Brothers and sisters in the Lord!" boomed J. P. Harrison. "I have travelled God's great southland long enough to learn that wherever a few of His children are gathered together, devil doubts and disbelief walk among us." Thick salt-and-pepper eyebrows lowered ominously when he stared into faces as if searching for signs of the devil.

His voice dropped. "Doubting Thomases lurk here even now, maybe sitting next to you." Silence descended on the crowd as individuals shot nervous glances to those seated at their sides.

"But the gospel truth . . ." the reverend's cry rang out. "The gospel truth is that God's work needs the support of Doubting Thomases, too! In a few moments, I'll tell you how each and every one of you assembled here tonight can lend a hand to the Lord's work. Right now, I want you to rejoice with me in God's Miracles."

With an actor's sense of timing, he waited, hands uplifted, for the swell of voices from the crowd to subside. Then he reached into the pulpit and pulled out a stack of newsprint. "*The Petersburg Republican, The Greenville Mountaineer, The Charleston Daily Courier*, all carry word of God's work on their front pages." Waving one of the papers, he roared, "I don't ask you to take my word for God's glory. Trust your own eyes, your own ears. Open your hearts to His greatness working among us."

The reverend pulled a pair of wire spectacles from his vest pocket and hooked them over his ears. Brandishing a news sheet, he read with reverence, " 'Miracle Miss Cured.' " Holding up a second paper, he intoned, " 'Miracle Worked Before Hundreds.' " Tone rising to full bellow, he cried, " 'Reverend Harrison Heals Blind Niece Before Charleston's Elite!' " He held the newspapers aloft while murmurs rippled through the assembly.

Dropping the sheets back onto the pulpit, the reverend spoke in a voice as soft as the night breeze. "But you, my brothers and sisters, *you* don't have to believe these fine newspapers. God's Miracle waits among us here in Cottonwood Creek, Texas, tonight. Open your hearts to proof of God's greatness, straight from one who personally knows His healing. Brothers and sisters, I give you my niece, Miss Morality Brown."

Zach sat up. He blinked his eyes, then looked again. My Lord, the gal could make a cowboy forget his horse.

The gray dress fit her like paper on the wall, displaying the kind of curves that made a man's mouth water. Yet, as bountiful as were her womanly gifts, the young lady who stood before the crowd was the very picture of wide-eyed innocence.

It was a nearly irresistible combination.

"Good evening." She folded her hands demurely and spoke in a strong, sincere voice. "I stand here before you to offer testimony of the miracle the Lord worked through the hands of my uncle, Reverend Harrison."

Zach's mouth lifted in a sardonic grin. Well, who'd have thought it? The gal was a hell of an actress. Lies and miracles, huh?

Everything was a scam.

"I was a young girl when an accident caused me to go blind," she declared. "For years I lived in a world of darkness, able to do little for myself, dependent upon others for the most simple things. I didn't even know my loved ones' faces. It was a sad and lonely existence, despite the efforts of my uncle and his wife, God rest her soul."

Keep tugging those heartstrings, sweet one, and their fingers will reach deeper into pockets.

Miss Brown glanced at him, and Zach lifted a brow at the nervousness she betrayed in that fleeting moment. She continued, "My uncle's work sent us from city to city, and in every one, my aunt would seek out the best doctors to examine my eyes. Time and again we were told to accept my condition as permanent. Following my aunt's untimely death, reality forced me to abandon hope of a cure."

She was good. Zach casually shifted in his seat to get a look at the folks sitting beside him. *Got 'em hooked, honey. Reel 'em in.*

Almost as if she'd heard him, she said, "Then, eight years ago in Charleston, West Virginia, a miracle happened. The day began as any other. My uncle set up his booth at a fair where he demonstrated the revolutionary new cleaning compound he had invented. I assisted as best I could, working mainly with a cotton cloth he used in the demonstrations. While I wasn't aware of it at the time, my uncle made it a practice to pray every day for my deliverance from affliction."

Pausing, she gifted the crowd with an angelic smile. "That spring morning, the Lord chose to answer his prayers."

Miss Brown reached for a cup atop a table behind

the pulpit, sipped at its contents, then returned it to its place. Zach nodded. Timing was right on the mark.

Her voice rang out on the cool night air. "I was sitting at a table, testing the texture of different squares of cloth and dividing them into stacks for my uncle's use. He visited with the city fathers a short distance away. I heard them conclude their conversation, and my uncle approached our booth." She shrugged her shoulders in an endearing, embarrassed manner and added, "He later told me he observed the mess I'd made of my task and silently asked the Lord to heal me."

Again Zach glanced nonchalantly over his shoulder. Many good folk were perched on the edge of their seats. By the looks of it, this hoax might work as well as any he'd seen during his days on the swindle circuit. He was impressed.

"The moments that followed are burned into my memory," Morality Brown declared with conviction. "I heard my uncle shout, 'God bless Morality.' He touched me, and from his hands, I felt a colossal force. It rocked me, an energy beyond description. Then, I saw a flash of brilliant, overpowering light, and I fainted."

She stopped and surveyed her audience, sincerity shining in round, moss-colored eyes. In a quiet voice filled with wonder and ringing with truth, she said, "And when I awoke, my sight had returned. I could see again."

"And now it's your turn to take part in God's marvelous works," Harrison declared. "Your hands, like mine, can be instruments of the Lord. I want every one of you to put a hand in his pocket or her purse. I want you to pull out the largest bill, the largest coin you have on you. I want your hands joined with mine in God's, to support the healing work the Lord Himself has empowered me to do."

The good people of Cottonwood Creek all but fell over themselves in their rush to add their contributions to the plate. Zach Burkett didn't bother to check the denomination of the coin he tossed in. He sat with his head cocked to one side, his gaze considering Morality Brown and the spectacle hosted by her uncle.

This gal was great, her uncle's show convincing.

How the hell could he use them?

Zach pondered the problem, standing with the others as they lifted their voices in "Just As I Am." Halfway through the first verse, a speculative smile spread across his face like honey on a hot roll. His bass voice boomed, joining the multitude in song.

Zach Burkett had seen the light.

And don't miss these electrifying
romances from Bantam Books,
on sale in June:

From *New York Times* best-selling author
Amanda Quick comes

MYSTIQUE
Amanda Quick "taps into women's
romantic fantasies with a master's touch."
—Janelle Taylor

VIOLET
by best-selling author

Jane Feather

"An author to treasure."
—*Romantic Times*

MOTHER LOVE
by acclaimed author

Judith Henry Wall

"Wall keeps you turning the pages."
—*San Francisco Chronicle Review*

WARLORD
by up-and-coming author

Elizabeth Elliott

DON'T MISS THESE FABULOUS BANTAM WOMEN'S FICTION TITLES

On sale in July

DEFIANT
by PATRICIA POTTER
Winner of the 1992 *Romantic Times*
Career Achievement Award for Storyteller of the Year

Only the desire for vengeance had spurred Wade Foster on, until the last of the men who had destroyed his family lay sprawled in the dirt. Now, badly wounded, the rugged outlaw closed his eyes against the pain . . . and awoke to the tender touch of the one woman who could show him how to live— and love—again. ____ 56601-6 $5.50/$6.99

STAR-CROSSED
by nationally bestselling author SUSAN KRINARD

"Susan Krinard was born to write romance."
—New York Times *bestselling author Amanda Quick*

A captivating futuristic romance in the tradition of Johanna Lindsey, Janelle Taylor, and Kathleen Morgan. A beautiful aristocrat risks a forbidden love . . . with a dangerously seductive man born of an alien race. ____ 56917-1 $4.99/$5.99

BEFORE I WAKE
by TERRY LAWRENCE

"Terry Lawrence is a magnificent writer." —Romantic Times
Award-winning author Terry Lawrence is an extraordinary storyteller whose novels sizzle with irresistible wit and high-voltage passion. Now, she weaves the beloved fairy tale *Sleeping Beauty* into a story so enthralling it will keep you up long into the night. ____ 56914-7 $5.50/$6.99

Ask for these books at your local bookstore or use this page to order.

Please send me the books I have checked above. I am enclosing $____ (add $2.50 to cover postage and handling). Send check or money order, no cash or C.O.D.'s, please.

Name _____

Address _____

City/State/Zip _____

Send order to: Bantam Books, Dept. FN159, 2451 S. Wolf Rd., Des Plaines, IL 60018
Allow four to six weeks for delivery.
Prices and availability subject to change without notice. FN 159 7/95